A BRIDE FOR BROTHERS, VOLUME 2

Wild Fascination
Keen Inclination

Abby Blake

LOVEXTREME FOREVER

Siren Publishing, Inc.
www.SirenPublishing.com

A SIREN PUBLISHING BOOK
IMPRINT: LoveXtreme Forever

A BRIDE FOR EIGHT BROTHERS, VOLUME 2
Wild Fascination
Keen Inclination
Copyright © 2011 by Abby Blake

ISBN-10: 1-61034-798-6
ISBN-13: 978-1-61034-798-3

First Printing: October 2011

Cover design by *Les Byerley*
All art and logo copyright © 2011 by Siren Publishing, Inc.

Printed in the U.S.A.

PUBLISHER
Siren Publishing, Inc.
www.SirenPublishing.com

DEDICATION

For Alexandra

Siren Publishing

LoveXtreme *Forever*

Wild Fascination

BOOK THREE

A Bride For Eight Brothers

Abby Blake

WILD FASCINATION

A Bride for Eight Brothers 3

ABBY BLAKE
Copyright © 2011

Chapter One

"Where the hell is he?" Mikayla asked angrily.

Brock had no idea where Lachlan was, and it was starting to piss him off. Mikayla wriggled her ass as much as she could considering she was tied down, and then growled in frustration.

When she had detailed her plan, Brock had obliged, mainly because he couldn't bear to see his wife upset. But now he had his sub facedown over Lachlan's spanking bench, her legs tied open, her ass and pussy just waiting to be spanked and fucked, and all he could do was sit here and wait for Lachlan to show his face. Shit! What was it they said about the best laid plans?

"Maybe you should go and look for him?" Mikayla suggested hopefully. He gave his woman an incredulous look that she probably didn't see. No. Fucking. Way. He had never left a sub unattended when she was tied down. There was no way he would start with his wife. The fact that she was laid out ready for Lachlan to whip her ass made Brock feel just a little bit insane. All this effort for Lachlan and the guy probably wouldn't even show up.

Brock sat beside Mikayla caressing her spine in long, sweeping strokes. She moaned quietly and mentioned Lachlan's name again.

Damn.

"Quiet, sub," he said, trying to hide his irritation. He wasn't jealous. He loved sharing his wife with his brothers, she was perfect for them, but it was starting to irritate him that Mikayla was trying so hard to get Lachlan's attention. For weeks now she'd been goading him, teasing him, taunting him and generally being an all out pain in the ass just to get him to spank her. Brock had even been quite impressed by Lachlan's refusal to be manipulated by their bratty sub until he'd noticed the man's lack of interest in everything else as well.

Lachlan hadn't been himself since learning of Mikayla's miscarriage, and even though Brock shared his disappointment, Lachlan seemed to be taking it to extremes. It was obvious that something more was going on in Lachlan's head, but Brock was certain his eldest brother would work it out in his own good time.

"Let me up," Mikayla demanded.

"No," Brock said in the most commanding voice he could muster.

"Brock, damn it, let me up so I can go find him." One hundred percent pure irritation slid into his mind. She was his sub and wife as much as she was Lachlan's, and unlike Lachlan, Brock didn't let his subs top from the bottom.

He moved around to stand in front of Mikayla. She lifted her head and looked him straight in the eye, and every dominant tendency roared to the surface.

"Eyes down, sub," he growled. She looked startled but quickly did as he said. He'd given her a lot of leeway since her pregnancy and miscarriage, but that was over. Either she was his sub or she wasn't, but he wouldn't let her pretend. He caressed the top of her head as she rested it on the spanking bench. She'd been tied this way for longer than he usually liked, but he needed to get a few things understood between them before he removed her bonds.

"Are you using your safe word, Mikayla?" She tried to lift her head again, but he held her still by her hair.

"No, S–Sir," she said in a trembling voice. He worried at her tone but continued to hold her immobile.

"Do you remember your safe word, sub?"

"Yes, Brock," she said in a stronger voice. Feeling a little more confident that he wasn't frightening her with his abrupt change in demeanor, Brock caressed her hair once more, allowing her to move her head slightly as she stretched to a more comfortable position.

"Tell me your safe word, Mikayla."

"Chipmunk, Sir." He smiled at his naughty sub, glad that she couldn't see his loss of control. The woman certainly knew how to push his buttons. She'd changed her safe word from red to chipmunk at the same time his brothers had been calling him by every animal name on this stupid icy rock of a planet. Just his luck he'd break a leg when the only medical help available was his smart-ass younger brothers who were veterinarians, not doctors. He couldn't wait to move on to their next contract. Two more weeks to finalize their data and forward the reports and recommendations, and they could pack up and get the hell off this fucked-up planet.

"No, sub," he said, feeling the need to correct Mikayla's bratty behavior, "your safe word is red. Is that understood?" He'd indulged her too long, and it was time to move back toward normal. And besides, being manipulated by his sub was not something he was ever willing to accept. Mikayla knew what he expected, had known since their very first time together, and he needed to get back to the relationship that made them both happy.

"Yes, Master," she said in a very submissive voice. His cock grew thicker with just those two soft words. She usually called him by his name, but when things between them started getting really intense, the word seemed to pop out of its own volition. Brock hoped this was her way of signaling that she understood his need.

"Good girl," he said as he caressed her neck and shoulders softly. "I'm going to undo your bonds. You can stretch and move your arms and legs, but I want you to stay lying facedown."

"Yes, Master." His cock twitched, pressing painfully against the zipper in his jeans.

He moved quickly, releasing her arms and legs and massaging the muscles to make certain that the blood was flowing properly. She moaned quietly as he released the straps just above her knees and helped her to move her legs. Brock caressed her inner thighs, pleased to feel her slick juices coating the skin.

"Baby girl," he said in a rough voice, "I need you."

* * * *

Mikayla swallowed hard. Brock was more intense than she'd ever seen him, and a small sliver of fear tickled down her spine. She knew he wouldn't ever hurt her—well, maybe a little of the good kind of hurt—but he took his responsibility to his sub very seriously and made every effort to be certain he never injured her. Just remembering some of the orgasms he'd coaxed from her made that small fear morph quickly into arousal and then overflow into desperate need.

He needed her? But, oh, how she needed him, too.

Brock had always been the most demanding of her husbands but also the most loving. After every session, he held her and pampered her, and always made her feel like she was the center of his universe.

She tried to stifle her moan as he lifted her from the spanking bench and draped her over his shoulder so that all the blood ran to her head. A moment later he placed her against the wall and tightened all of the straps into place. The last one went around her waist and she shivered in anticipation knowing that Brock only used that restraint when he expected the session to be long and intense.

He stood behind her, his warm hand caressing her ass. "Are you comfortable, sub?"

"Yes, Master," she replied, trying to hide the warble in her voice. She could already feel her pussy pulsing in anticipation. Her cream slid down her thighs, the tangy smell of her arousal filling the room.

"Count for me, sub. Twenty to warm up."

The leather flogger caressed the skin on her ass, gliding slowly over her flesh. He lifted it away and bought it down against her, the delicious sting already playing havoc with her thought processes.

"One," she finally remembered to say. A second followed quickly, and she bit back the demand for more. Brock would gag her, no hesitation, if she started making demands now. At this moment, he was her Master, and she needed to curtail her impulses. The fact that she hated the O-ring he used as a gag was deterrent enough to stay quiet, for now.

Her ass and thighs were starting to heat as his lashes took on more force. She counted automatically, barely aware of the numbers coming from her mouth, her concentration turning inward as desire flooded her veins. She shook as the final slap of the flogger grazed her pussy. Her knees gave out, her weight falling against the brace around her middle.

Brock caressed her tender flesh with his warm, work-roughened hand for a moment before moving into her line of sight. "Are you comfortable, sub?" She was buzzing with adrenaline, shaking with arousal, and about to have an incredible orgasm, and he wanted to know if she was comfortable? Seriously?

"Yes, Master," she managed to get out when she finally remembered how to talk.

"I have a new toy," he said, caressing her jaw with his fingers. "I believe you're ready to try it, sub." She nodded even knowing that he wasn't asking her permission. If she wanted him to stop, she just had to use her safe word, but she was so close to orgasm the last thing she wanted was for him to stop. She heard him rummage around in one of the closets, and then he was back, standing behind her, caressing her bottom for a moment.

"You have a beautiful ass, sub. I love seeing it this color. Count them for me. We'll start with ten."

She stayed very still. Not knowing what Brock held in his hand was disconcerting. Last time he'd done this, she'd been introduced to a thick strip of leather. Brock had left a beautiful row of stripes on her ass and given her the most incredible of orgasms, but she hadn't been able to sit comfortably for several days.

She had a feeling that whatever he had now was going to be even more intense.

Whatever it was hit her ass with such force that she grunted in pain. He rubbed over the spot slowly with his hand, obviously admiring the reddened skin. She closed her eyes against the tears that threatened to escape. Her ass had begun to throb just from one blow, and he expected her to take ten for starters? Her safe word was on her lips but the number one came out instead.

The second blow hit her other cheek, and she sucked in a breath at the painful sensation. She squirmed against the wall, her body trying to protect her even when her mind begged for more. "Two," she said, trying not to clench her cheeks in anticipation of the next blow.

The third and fourth came quickly, the fifth even harder, and then the pain morphed into more. Her orgasm started as the sixth blow landed. She was barely aware of Brock counting the rest for her as every nerve ending buzzed, and her brain shut down to anything but the incredible sensations spiraling through her.

She barely registered the removal of her bonds but fell into Brock's embrace before she could hit the ground. He swung her into his arms, carried her back to the spanking bench, placed her facedown, and entered her pussy in one long, hard thrust.

She squeaked as her second orgasm burst. Brock grabbed her hips, pressed her against the bench, ground her clit against the soft leather, and pounded into her harder and harder and harder. Gasping, squirming, begging, Mikayla took everything he had to give and wanted more.

She felt him swell, her pussy lips convulsing around his hard length, and then he pushed deeper into her, holding her down as he filled her with his seed. For long moments he just held her there, breathing hard against her back, his cock twitching inside her.

* * * *

Shit. What had he done? The woman had suffered a miscarriage only a few months ago.

He'd been so desperate for her that he'd forgotten and nearly lost control. Nearly. It had taken every ounce of strength he'd had left to undo her bonds and move her to a more comfortable position before he fucked her like a wild thing. He'd been so close to cramming his cock into her back passage and taking her against the wall that he shook a little with the realization. Fucking her ass without lube or preparation likely would've been very painful for her and possibly resulted in injury. He wasn't pleased with his train of thought.

He lifted away from her, acknowledging that in his desperate need to claim her he'd probably pressed a little too hard against her back as well. God, he hoped she'd forgive him. He lifted her into his arms, cradling her high against his chest as he studied her face. Tears streaked her skin, her eyes red and watery, but she gave him a contented sigh and practically purred as she nestled in his arms.

God, he loved this woman.

He placed her gently on the bed and then went to run a cool bath. Her ass would likely be very sore for a few hours, and he intended to make sure he cared for his sub properly.

"Thank you," she whispered as he turned to leave. He turned back wanting to be certain why she was thanking him. After all, he had promised the ten hits with the paddle were for starters. Maybe she was thanking him for *not* following through on that. Judging by the small hiss of pain as he'd lowered her to the bed, Brock suspected that ten was about all she could take.

When he raised an eyebrow, she smiled and explained.

"Thank you for treating me like you used to. Everyone has been tiptoeing around me since the miscarriage, and it feels really lovely to be treated like I'm not about to shatter into a million little pieces."

He shook his head. Had they really been treating her differently? They'd been very concerned for her, both emotionally and physically, but had he and his brothers treated her so differently that she'd felt unloved? A shiver racked through him as he realized that he really had treated her differently. Hell, he'd been ready to sit her on his knee and feed her—something he knew she absolutely hated—just because he'd treated her roughly. Nothing they'd done today was any more painful or any less pleasurable than their most intense sessions before she'd fallen pregnant.

"I'm sorry," he said as he settled on the edge of the bed and touched her face. "I guess we've been a little overzealous trying to protect you. I promise to try harder to get our relationship back to what it was before."

She smiled sweetly, obviously relieved that he understood her needs.

He moved away, back into the bathroom and began to run a cool bath. His sub was precious, loving, independent, and strong, and when she gave him her trust like she'd done today, there was no greater gift. He planned never to take it for granted again.

"When do we move to the new research station?" she asked from the doorway.

"What? Tired of this messed-up planet already?" he teased. Considering that the men outnumbered women by three hundred to one, and Mikayla had been dumped here by a people-trafficking ring, he probably shouldn't be making jokes. Add that to the fact pregnancy was outlawed but rape was not and that it was the coldest motherfucker of a planet he'd ever been on, it was a pretty safe bet none of them would mourn the need to leave it behind.

Mikayla smiled as if she knew what he was thinking then moved into his embrace as she waited for his answer.

"We have about ten days worth of reporting left to do, and then we can pack up the station—most of it comes with us—and head for the jungles of M789zi."

"What are the laws like?" she asked, sounding slightly apprehensive. Shit, who could blame her? A man who'd claimed to love her had abandoned her on this planet. Fortunately, Matt had been there to rescue Mikayla from her first client and would-be rapist and had brought her here to their research station. It was only natural that she'd want to know of the laws of the new planet. Although, Brock doubted any planet could be as fucked-up as this one.

"There aren't any people on the new planet, so there are no actual laws. Basically, it will be you and me and your other seven husbands."

She hugged him harder, seeming quite pleased by that assurance.

* * * *

After a soothing bath, Mikayla curled into her husband's warmth, snuggling closer as thoughts of the next planet filled her head. It felt wonderful to lie here exhausted, sated, and loved. She'd missed this more than she realized. Brock had been attentive and caring since her miscarriage but the pampering always felt a little awkward. There was nothing quite like the exhaustion that followed an intense spanking session and amazing orgasms. She felt weak and vulnerable, and it made Brock's care for her seem so much more special.

She just hoped they'd be able to move past the problem now. She wasn't fragile, and she was glad Brock finally realized it.

Of course she still had seven other husbands who needed to know the same thing.

Chapter Two

"Hello, sweetheart," Ryan said as he walked into the lab, "what are you doing in here so late?"

"I just wanted to make sure everything is finished before we start packing up tomorrow." It was a plausible excuse but not entirely the truth. As weird as it sounded, even to her own ears, she was going to miss this place. Everything good that had ever happened to her had happened on this base, and even though her arrival on this planet had been unexpected and terrifying, it had led to her being happier than she'd ever imagined possible.

Somehow, Mikayla Noone, the girl that no one wanted, ended up being loved by eight incredible, amazing men. And most of that had happened here. It was the coldest, most fucked-up planet she could ever imagine, but still it felt like home.

"What's that look for?" Ryan asked quietly. Damn. The trouble with having eight husbands was that sooner or later they were going to figure out what was going on in her head.

"Just a little nervous, I guess." She shrugged, trying to give the impression that it didn't matter. Ryan didn't buy it. He pulled her into his embrace, rested his head on top of hers and somehow saw directly into her heart.

"You're going to miss this place." She nodded against his chest, half-relieved that he knew and half-worried he wouldn't understand. "Did you know," he asked quietly as he pulled her closer, "that the entire station gets moved? About the only thing we'll leave on this planet is some foundation supports. Everything else pulls apart like a jigsaw puzzle, and when we get to the next planet, it all gets put back together."

"Seriously?" It wasn't that she wanted to call him a liar, but, well, Ryan was known for goofing around, and it seemed just a little too incredible. The whole base? At the moment it housed nine adults, office space, living quarters, storage areas, and the lab. It wasn't a large building, but it certainly didn't fit her idea of a mobile home.

"Seriously," he said in a reassuring voice and a tighter cuddle. "Everything will look exactly the same on the next planet. In fact, if you stayed inside the lab or the living quarters the whole time, you wouldn't even know we were on another planet."

That gave her a small measure of peace. She was taking her husbands and her home to the next planet, so it was hardly a move at all. But she hugged Ryan tighter just in case.

"Damn," Ty said as he came into the room. "I was hoping to find you alone, so we could run off on our holiday and leave the extras behind." Mikayla laughed at his words. Ty would never actually consider a holiday without at least Ryan with them, but he did enjoy teasing his brothers. Fortunately, Ryan was immune to his words.

"Is Peter ready to go?"

"Yep," Ty said as he glanced around the lab. "We're all set to leave in the morning. Unfortunately, Matt and Bryce are insisting you stay your last night here with them. I tried to explain that we will be really busy on the next planet and that we needed to spend every moment with you until then, but sadly they disagreed."

Mikayla was on the verge of laughter when Ty's words finally struck her as odd. "Wait. I though the planet was uninhabited. What will keep us so busy?"

"Uninhabited by humanoids or sentient species according to the advance survey team, but there's plenty of life on the planet. Bugs, insects, spiders, creepy-crawlies." Ty said it like she should go all girlie and react with a squeal, but she just raised an eyebrow. After her experiences, she was far more frightened of humans than tiny little insects.

"Okay," she said slowly as she tried again to convince herself that a holiday would be all right. Ryan and Ty worked really hard, so they definitely deserved some time off. "So, uhm, where are we going?"

"Well, Peter has appointments on Earth for a few days, so we'll go see Tracey and make a decision from there." Mikayla nodded, feeling a little more enthusiastic. Speaking to Tracey once a week wasn't quite the same as seeing her face-to-face. Despite the woman's reassurances, Mikayla wasn't convinced that Tracey was over the whole *nearly abducted and sold into prostitution* thing, so checking in on her was a pretty good idea.

"Okay," she said, starting to feel just a little bit excited now. "Tracey lives in California these days. It's summer there, too, so maybe we can spend some time on the beach."

Ty and Ryan seemed quite happy with that.

"Come on, darlin'," Ty said as he held a hand out for her. "Let's go contact Tracey and see if she can recommend a luxury hotel nearby."

"Luxury?" she asked, feeling just a little uneasy. Would that word ever mean anything good in her mind again? It had been the one word Jet had used over and over as he promised her the world and then dumped her on a planet where the only way for a woman to survive was by prostitution. She tried to hide the shudder, but Ty felt it anyway.

God, what was wrong with her? She'd been off the planet before—except of course that was when she uncovered a human trafficking ring, discovered her pregnancy, got left behind on Earth because pregnant women weren't allowed on this planet, and then had a frightening miscarriage. Of course it had also been when she saved Tracey, met Bryce, and forged a deeper understanding with Matt. So, her last trip to Earth wasn't all bad, but she was still in no hurry to repeat the experience.

Ty must've guessed her thought process because he pulled her closer and whispered, "We'll be beside you the whole time. I promise, no matter where you go, you will have at least two husbands by your side."

Tears filmed her eyes as she nodded. It annoyed the hell out of her to feel so insecure—despite her loving husbands' reassurances—but she couldn't seem to shake it. She just hoped that when things settled back into routine on the new planet that she could regain that sense of peace she'd discovered here on this icy mining planet.

Even knowing where the irrational feeling came from hadn't really helped her to overcome it. She'd spent most of her younger years being shuffled from one foster family to another, so continuity was something she now seemed desperate to hold on to.

"Maybe we could stay with Tracey," Ryan said evenly. Mikayla smiled at that idea. It was one thing to drop in on a friend. It was quite another to bring three husbands with her. And besides, it would be quite pleasant to stay in a hotel. Maybe a smaller, less luxurious hotel than Ty had in mind, but something close to Tracey so that they could visit every day would be nice.

"Let's call Tracey," she said, determined to ignore the hard thumping of her heart as anxiety swelled through her once more. She ground her teeth together. God, she was going to get this annoying fear under control if it was the last thing she did. "I'm sure she can recommend something to suit us."

Ty smiled, still looking concerned, but she grinned back and forced herself to relax. It was going to be all right. She would have Ryan, Ty, and Peter by her side, so she had nothing to fear but fear itself.

Now, if she could just unclench her jaw.

* * * *

The hotel was quite surprising. Small enough to have a friendly feel to it and classy enough that no one raised an eyebrow when Mrs. Davidson checked in with three husbands. Their suite had three rooms, two with double beds and the main with a king-size. Everything seemed clean, well maintained, and comfortable.

"What shall we do first?" Ryan asked as he carried all of their suitcases into the main room. Peter had some sort of business in New York and would join them in a couple of days, so for now she'd share the main room with the twins.

"I'd like to visit Tracey, but I think I need time to recover from traveling," Mikayla said as she sat in the seat and kicked off her shoes. She'd spent almost all of her time at the station barefoot, so having to put on shoes—even comfortable sandals—was proving to be more difficult than she'd expected. She'd love one of Lachlan's foot rubs about now, but there was no way she was going to say that out loud. The last time Ryan and Ty had given her a foot rub they'd made her laugh so hard she'd almost fallen off the sofa. She definitely didn't have the energy for excessive giggling at the moment.

"Okay," Ty said, taking a seat beside her, "Tracey's place is only a few blocks from here, so we could probably walk." She tried to hide the grimace behind a smile, but he noticed it anyway.

"Sore feet?" he asked, sounding very hopeful.

"No," she said quickly, moving to sit on them before he could get any ideas. Ty grinned but made no move toward her.

"Maybe we should have a nap first," Ryan said, wiggling his eyebrows suggestively. She laughed at his antics. A nap sounded wonderful, but with these two she was unlikely to do any actual sleeping. "Or maybe," he said, stalking closer, "we can play around and then have a nap."

She smiled as he lifted her straight off the sofa and into his arms. Mikayla didn't need to look back to know that Ty was right behind them. By the time they had her naked, they'd kissed just about every inch of flesh she owned.

Writhing in the middle of the bed as Ryan licked her pussy and Ty suckled her breasts suddenly seemed like the best idea they'd had in months. She tried to lift her hips to force Ryan's tongue deeper, but he pulled away and laughed at her impatience.

"Sweetheart," he admonished, "we need to do this properly if you're going to get the right type of sleep." She rolled her eyes at his teasing.

"Please, Ryan, I need you inside me."

"Well, since you asked so nicely." He surged over her, his cock thrusting hard and deep in a single movement. Ty laughed as his brother held still, pinning her to the bed and refusing to move. She growled at his literal interpretation of her words.

"I think," Ty said with a huge grin on his face, "maybe you needed to be more specific."

"Fine," she said, rolling her eyes and bucking her hips against Ryan's hold. "Please fuck me." His eyes darkened as he began to move leisurely. He slid in and out of her pussy, the slow glide and gentle rhythm surprising in its appeal. Ty leaned over and kissed her just as calmly, the soft press of his lips against hers quite satisfying.

Ryan pulled away but Ty quickly took his place, slowly riding her as pressure built rapidly despite their gentle loving. She began to breathe deeper, more rapidly, and Ty started moving faster. She was squirming, trying to get closer when he pulled away and let Ryan take over. Ryan slammed into her, his balls slapping her ass as her arousal spiked, and she started to shake. Over and over he fucked her, his hands grabbing her buttocks and lifting her to him, forcing her to take more. He changed the angle. Ty found her clit with his finger, circling, pressing, grinding against the hard button until she screamed her release.

Ryan pounded into her harder, his breathing labored as he groaned his own release. Again, he pulled away and Ty took over, thrusting deep into her quivering pussy, setting off a second, more intense climax. Mikayla moaned as she felt him hit his peak and release his seed into her body as well.

After a few slower, gentler strokes, Ty finally stilled inside her. They lay together, still joined as he softly kissed her jaw. "I love you," he whispered.

"So do I," Ryan said from beside them as he caressed her face and swept the hair from her eyes. "Rest now."

She nodded sleepily, quite willing to follow orders. "I love you," she mumbled to them both as Ty moved to her side and encouraged her to lay her head on his shoulder. She barely had the energy to roll over.

* * * *

"She's asleep already," Ty said softly. "I think traveling really wears her out. Or should I say," he said with a concerned frown, "the anxiety travel causes wears her out."

Ryan nodded in agreement. It was obvious that Mikayla didn't like change. She'd been jittery for the last month at the research station and, despite his and Ryan's and Peter's reassurances, was still uneasy about taking this holiday. He knew her last visit to Earth hadn't been entirely pleasant, but something told him it was more than that. Mikayla rarely mentioned anything of her life before meeting him and his brothers, so it was quite possible the reason ran a lot deeper.

Lately, Ty had found himself wondering more and more about their wife's past, but he genuinely hoped Mikayla would simply explain it to them when she felt comfortable enough. It wasn't as if any of them had asked her a direct question about her childhood, so she wasn't deliberately hiding something, she just hadn't offered any information freely. They knew she had no living relatives, but that was about the sum total of their knowledge. Ty couldn't help but shudder at the idea of having no family. Having grown up with seven brothers and five parents, his life had always been filled with many, many people.

There had been times when he'd wished for a little peace and quiet, but he'd always known that when he needed his family, they would be there for him. A touch of guilt slipped through his mind as he thought of how awful it must have been for Bryce. Even though Bryce had assured them all that it had been his choice at the time, Ty couldn't miss just how happy Bryce was now with his brothers and Mikayla.

* * * *

Ryan rolled over, feeling agitated. "I'll go check the messages. I'm hoping that Peter has some good news. I can't believe that bitch is trying to sue him." He didn't bother putting clothes back on, just headed for the communication equipment provided with the room. Most people on Earth still used personal mobile phones, but having spent very little time on their home planet in recent years, neither he nor his brothers had felt the need. It would've come in handy about now, though. Waiting for a message via the global networks was a pain in the ass.

As soon as Ryan logged on, Peter's message flashed up. It wasn't marked urgent, but that didn't really mean anything. Peter said he would handle the situation, so it was unlikely he'd be sending an SOS for help. His message was short and succinct. "Not much to report. Nothing has changed. The lawyers are still arguing, and Jessie won't back down. I'll let you know if the damn thing goes to court, but at this stage it looks likely."

Ryan didn't like the sound of that. He didn't know much about Peter and his ex-fiancée, but he did know that she'd hurt his brother pretty badly. So badly that Peter had nearly walked away from Mikayla for fear of being hurt again. Fortunately Mikayla with her loving heart and quiet acceptance had overcome his doubts, and now

Peter was as happy as the rest of them. At least he would be if he didn't have a potential lawsuit hanging over him.

Ryan headed back into the bedroom and simply stood beside the bed watching his wife sleep in his brother's arms. Ty opened his eyes and Ryan shook his head. "No change," he said quietly. "The bitch is still after his money."

Ty shook his head slowly, obviously as disgusted by the frivolous lawsuit as Ryan felt.

"I'm going to grab a shower and order some lunch." Ty nodded and then closed his eyes again, but Ryan could see the tension in his brother's jaw. They were all on edge over this damn lawsuit, but so far they'd managed to keep the news from Mikayla. They were trying to protect her from worry, but more than once Ryan wondered if they were doing the right thing.

As he stepped into the shower, he wondered how quickly his lovely wife would castrate them all if she found out they were keeping secrets.

Chapter Three

Tracey looked really well. Mikayla had talked to her at least once a week since the thwarted attempt to abduct her several months ago, but she'd worried that Tracey had been putting on a brave face. Considering how wonderful she looked, Mikayla's concerns seemed unfounded.

"I'd like you to meet someone," Tracey said nervously as she grabbed Mikayla's hand and dragged her into the living area. "This is my," she hesitated, glanced at the man, blushed, and then said, "my…um…friend, Rick. I live here with him and his brothers, Tony and Ashton."

Rick looked amused at the introduction but smiled and waved hello. He greeted Ryan and Ty with a handshake, offered them a cold beer, and led them onto the back veranda.

Mikayla smiled. She'd never been slow on the uptake, and she raised an eyebrow in question. Tracey's face colored even more, but she nodded slowly. "Does that shock you?"

Mikayla couldn't hold back the laugh. "You're talking to a woman who has eight husbands. I don't think my best friend sleeping with three men is going to shock me.

Tracey looked very relieved, and Mikayla had to wonder how many people had reacted poorly to Tracey's choice of partners. It still shocked Mikayla that people could be so narrow-minded. Despite the fact that polygamy for both men and women had been legal for generations, some people just had to victimize anyone who didn't think the way they did.

"I'm sorry about your miscarriage," Tracey said kindly. "Have you thought anymore about trying again?"

Mikayla smiled, knowing that Tracey only raised the issue because she was concerned for her. Mikayla hadn't quite been able to hide her fear of becoming pregnant again from another woman. Tracey was also a nurse, so she probably had experience dealing with people who'd suffered unexpected loss.

In some ways Mikayla felt her grief was a little silly. She'd barely been pregnant and had only known for a few weeks. One of the doctors had even—rather tactlessly—explained that the ectopic pregnancy would never have grown into a fully developed baby, so she hadn't really lost a child at all.

But it felt like she had. It felt like there was a hole in her heart where her love for her child would've been, and she couldn't quite find the courage to risk going through all that again. Her husbands were very supportive of her decision to put things off for a while, but sooner or later she would have to face it or risk never having children. Her men would make wonderful fathers, and they deserved the chance to try again, so she knew she couldn't be a coward forever.

"I'll talk to them all when we get settled on the new planet," she said, trying very hard not to shake. Tracey looked pleased. Even though most of their friendship had been over subspace communication, Mikayla was very glad for the woman's understanding and quiet support.

Hopefully—Mikayla thought as she threaded her arm through Tracey's and headed out to the veranda to join the men—Rick, Tony, and Ashton were worthy of Tracey's love, and they would be able to build a happy life together. Tracey was a complete sweetheart, and she deserved to be loved properly.

Tracey took a seat next to her lover and snuggled into the man's embrace. Rick smiled happily. "Does this mean the secret's out?" Tracey smiled shyly, but Mikayla didn't miss the adoration in her eyes. She seemed truly happy, and after everything that had happened, it was so lovely to see. Mikayla suddenly felt really glad they'd come to visit.

She snuggled between Ryan and Ty, feeling more relaxed than she had in weeks.

* * * *

"When did Peter say he was going to get here?" It had been three days, and she was sure he'd been intending to join them in two.

"Maybe tomorrow," Ty said.

"Maybe?" she asked as suspicion niggled into her brain. Both Ryan and Ty had been quick to trivialize Peter's need to be in New York, but the fact that he hadn't joined them when he was supposed to certainly suggested he was dealing with something that wasn't as unimportant as her husbands had led her to believe.

"He just has one more meeting, and then he'll be here," Ryan said, looking just a little bit uncomfortable.

"What about?" Every impulse was telling her she was missing something. She asked the question in a casual voice, yet her need to know was anything but.

"Oh, you know," Ty said, looking very uncomfortable. "Business and contract stuff."

"Doesn't John handle all that?" She was definitely smelling deception now. When they both looked unable to answer, she knew her instincts were spot on. "Okay, Mr. Davidson, spill. Why is Peter really in New York?"

"Maybe Peter should tell you himself," Ryan said, looking more uncomfortable than she'd ever seen him.

"Maybe you should tell me, and I can decide for myself if Peter should've told me." She crossed her arms and waited. Damn it all to hell. She knew they probably believed they were protecting her, but not knowing what was going on with one of her husbands was far worse.

"Sweetheart," Ryan said in an attempt to placate her.

"Don't you sweetheart me! Explain it to me, Ryan. I am your wife, and I demand to know what the hell is going on."

Ty stepped forward. He looked like he was about to embrace her but changed his mind when he saw her fierce expression. "Mikayla, it's nothing serious. Peter is just having some trouble with his ex-fiancée." He must've realized by the steam ready to come out of her ears that he'd phrased that very, very badly. "I mean," he said, quickly correcting himself, "the woman is trying to sue him for breach of promise for calling off the engagement. If he's seen her at all, it will have been on the opposite side of the negotiation table while their lawyers argue."

Finally, she let Ty pull her into his arms, but so many questions buzzed through her head that she didn't quite know where to start. "Breach of promise? I thought she was the one to call off the engagement? How could she be suing him?"

"We're not sure, darlin'," Ty said as he ran his hand up and down her spine in a soothing motion. "But it would seem that none of us got the full story of what happened between them."

"I want to talk to him." They both looked wary but eventually nodded, and Ty headed toward the communicator.

"No," she said quickly, "face-to-face. How long will it take to get to New York?"

Ty quickly called up the local transport schedule. "Looks like the new sky-pods run every two hours. The trip takes less than an hour. If we catch the next one, we can be there before his next meeting starts."

She nodded decisively. They were going to New York.

* * * *

Peter sat in the coffee shop downstairs from his hotel room. He scrubbed a hand over his face as he mentally went over everything his lawyer had told him in the past three days. When he'd broken his engagement to Jessie, Peter had no idea this type of civil suit was even possible. The woman was going after everything he owned and then some. She'd even managed to make his suggestion that he share her with his brothers somehow seem like she'd been engaged to all of them. Peter's lawyer was actually quite concerned because if she somehow proved that, she could basically go after all of their assets.

Damn. He'd called off the engagement because Jessie had demanded he hand over the family business in exchange for sleeping with his brothers. It had felt so cold, so calculating, and certainly not the loving relationship he'd envisioned for him or his brothers. Peter couldn't imagine the gall it took to go after the family business when she'd never actually been part of the family.

He closed his eyes as images of the woman who did love him filled his mind. Mikayla was everything he'd ever hoped for. She loved him and his brothers equally, had never asked for anything more than their love in return, and had actively assisted in their family business wherever she'd been able to help.

Mikayla was the woman who completed him. Not just him, but all of his brothers. She'd even seen into Bryce's soul and managed to bring him home where he belonged. Yet if Peter's ex-fiancée had her way, she'd make sure Mikayla was homeless with the rest of them.

Damn. He missed his wife more each minute. The reminder of the woman who'd claimed to love him but had only been interested in money made Mikayla seem even more precious. He'd nearly decided to skip the afternoon's negotiations just so he could go to California and visit his wife when an angel's voice called his name.

His eyes flew open to see the most amazing mirage, and then she was in his arms, kissing him, holding him, reminding him of everything that was good in his world.

"Mikayla," he breathed on a sigh. He glanced up to see Ryan and Ty behind her, but he couldn't even be mad that they'd brought her to him. No matter how complicated the lawsuit was becoming, he was very glad to see his wife. She snuggled into his arms, and he held her tight.

"You should've told me," she said quietly. He couldn't deny that. He should've told her. He'd wanted to protect her from the ugliness of his ex-fiancée's ambitions, but selfishly he needed her close.

"I'm sorry, Mikayla. I should've told you."

"You should've," she agreed, "but the three of us will be beside you for this afternoon's meeting." He opened his mouth to protest her involvement, but she put a hand over his lips to stop the words. "And we'll talk about honesty later. Right now I need my wayward husband to make love to me."

Ryan and Ty's faces lit up with excitement, but Peter was quick to douse that idea. He might share his wife with his brothers, but he wasn't about to share her in his bed. They both gave him rueful looks, indicating that they knew full well his thoughts on that matter, but they smiled and indicated for him to lead the way.

Peter sent his brothers a nod of gratitude and then lifted his beautiful wife to her feet. They held each other close as they headed to his hotel room. It still didn't feel quite real as he left his brothers in the living area and took his wife into his hotel bedroom. She kissed him all over as he tried to strip her of clothes. He carefully levered her shoes off and kissed the red marks where they'd rubbed her skin raw.

Mikayla was so beautiful in such a natural way that he couldn't imagine anything more perfect than his wife pregnant and barefoot. It was such a sexist attitude that he didn't voice it out loud, but he hoped that one day soon he could convince her to try again. He could understand her reluctance after the miscarriage and was more than willing to give her time, but he loved the idea of her as the mother of his children.

She sighed as he lifted her onto the bed and began worshipping every part of her he could reach. He dipped his head to taste her honeyed warmth and massaged her thighs as they began to quiver. She tilted her hips higher, demanding more, and he gave it to her, unable to deny her anything. She rode his tongue, her hands fisted in his hair, her pussy slick and swollen. She moaned when her orgasm hit and he gentled her with soothing, long strokes of his tongue.

She tugged his hair, and he moved up her body, fitting his cock against her entrance, pressing in slowly as he watched her face. She held him with her body, trapped his heart with her love and ensnared his soul for all time.

When his orgasm came, he sighed at the perfection of the moment and caressed his wife's lovely face. She smiled sleepily and he rolled onto his back, pulling her over him, staying inside her where he belonged.

It wasn't long before Ryan and Ty woke him, so he could attend the negotiation, but this time he wasn't going alone. This time he had his family to support him.

* * * *

Mikayla's first glimpse of the woman who would sue her husband was disconcerting. Dressed in a formal power suit with high heels and perfectly styled hair, Jessie Evans made Mikayla feel more than a little underdressed. Mikayla glanced down at her simple cotton sundress and smoothed a wrinkle from the front with her slightly shaking hand.

Maybe this was a really bad idea. Peter had spent the last hour arguing that she should stay at the hotel with Ryan and Ty. When she'd explained that her place was at her husband's side, he'd tried to order her to stay behind. That hadn't gone down very well. She might enjoy being submissive in bed, but that didn't mean she would let her men dictate her life outside of the bedroom.

She swallowed nervously, tried to find the courage she thought she possessed, and quietly listened to the conversations going on around her. The woman smiled at her, the expression far from friendly, and Mikayla tried not to feel even more intimidated.

Even though Peter held her hand in a comforting grip, and Ryan and Ty stood off to her left, Mikayla couldn't quite shake the cold contempt she sensed from Peter's ex. The woman's smirk certainly seemed derogatory. She looked Mikayla over for another moment, apparently assessing her potential as a rival, and then dismissed her just as quickly. To say the woman was extremely intimidating was probably an understatement.

What Mikayla couldn't quite understand was how Peter would've ever considered himself in love with her. The woman gave off a vibe that surely every other person in the room could sense. Or maybe not. Mikayla was the only other woman in the room. The men seemed oblivious to Jessie's malice. Mikayla glanced away, trying not to look in the woman's direction. A moment later she realized her mistake.

"Ryan, Ty, how lovely to see you again."

"Again?" Ryan said, sounding startled. "I've never even met you."

"Oh, darling, how you wound me. Peter is being positively arctic, but I never expected you two to reject me as well." The woman did a good job of looking stricken, but Mikayla could see through the ruse even if the lawyers couldn't. Everyone in the room watched the exchange closely. The woman's lawyer even smiled slightly as Jessie Evans played the jilted lover to a waiting crowd. "Peter even brought a date to our reconciliation talks. I've tried so hard to have him love me, but he couldn't be more callous if he'd taken a knife to my breast."

Mikayla rolled her eyes. She may have felt intimidated by the well-groomed bitch, but the woman was laying it on a bit thick. Reconciliation talks?

"Is that what you're calling it now?" Peter asked disdainfully. "Reconciliation? It sure feels like you're trying to sue me for everything I have. That's not reconciliation in my book."

"Well, I can see by the little homewrecker attached to your arm that you have no intentions of trying to settle our differences, so I have no choice but to protect myself and ensure my financial future." The sweet smile the woman managed chilled Mikayla to the bone. It was the sort of smile a predator wore when the prey had nowhere else to go.

Peter's lawyer stepped up to him, urging him not to engage in any more conversation, but Peter seemed unable to walk away from such obvious lies. "Mikayla is not a home wrecker, she's my wife. I met her nearly two years after you and I broke up." The look of interest in the woman's eyes was quite chilling. Obviously she'd heard something she liked. "And as to your financial future, I suggest you go find some rich fool to hand over his money and leave me and my family alone."

The woman did it perfectly. Her bottom lip quivered, her shoulders shook, a strangled gasp escaped her perfectly made up lips, and then she managed to rush from the room while looking both heartbroken and distressed without getting a hair out of place. Displaying concern Mikayla doubted they actually felt, her lawyer and several others followed.

Peter's lawyer shook his head. "I really wish you hadn't said that."

Peter shrugged, clearly not concerned by his lawyer's wish. The man turned his attention to Mikayla. "Are you married only to Peter?" She shook her head as Peter became very still. "How many brothers are you married to?"

"All of them," she answered in a small voice. What the hell was going on? Polygamy was legal. Granted, eight husbands was unusual, but it was certainly no crime.

"Damn, Peter, I really wish you hadn't said that."

"Why?" Ryan asked as he stepped forward to take Mikayla's other hand in his own.

"Because now Ms. Evans has reasonable proof that your engagement was a promise to marry all of you. I can practically guarantee that her lawyer is tracking down your marriage certificates as we speak. This could get really ugly."

Peter nodded his head, his hand squeezing Mikayla's tighter, as the gravity of what he'd done seemed to sink in. Mikayla wanted to reassure him that Jessie probably would've found out about their marriage anyway, but it was probably best for her to remain silent now and listen to what their lawyer was saying.

"Contact your brothers. We need to consider offering some sort of settlement. If this gets to court, she could very well win half of all of yours and your brother's assets and maybe even a yearly alimony payment."

"But she's never even met us," Ryan said through his tightly clenched teeth. The lawyer just shook his head.

"It will come down to your word against hers. Even if you can prove that you've never met her, she'll just claim that Peter was speaking for all of you." The lawyer grabbed his notepad and started packing his briefcase. "I'll speak to her counsel on the way out, but I'm sure they won't be back at the negotiating table today. They'll want to gather every bit of information they can, so they can claim a huge payout. You should expect a particularly unpleasant day tomorrow."

* * * *

Ryan couldn't quite believe he was being sued by a woman he'd never even met, let alone that she was suing him for breaking an engagement he hadn't been a part of. Hell, from what their lawyer had said, the woman's claim was not only solid but likely to cost them plenty if it ever got before a judge.

"We need to contact the others," Peter said tiredly, "and let them know the mess I dragged them into."

"Peter," Mikayla said softly, her heart obviously breaking for him. "This isn't your fault. You have every right to search for love. Just because she wasn't the right woman for you doesn't mean you did anything wrong." He didn't look convinced. "We are a family. We'll get through this as a family. Okay?" He nodded. "No more secrets. We need to know exactly what's happening. Where did she get the idea to claim she was engaged to all of you?"

Peter looked uncomfortable but managed to force the words past his throat. "Because I asked her to consider meeting my brothers and maybe sharing their beds."

Ryan didn't think he could be any more surprised than he was at the meeting. Turned out he was wrong. Peter had wanted to share a wife even before they'd met Mikayla? It seemed so far out of the realms of possibility that Ryan had to look to his twin for confirmation. Ty just shrugged, clearly as astonished as Ryan.

"But she never met them?"

"She met John, who didn't say if he liked her or not, and Matt, who disliked her immediately, but not the others. I think she just got lucky today with Ty and Ryan because she knows my youngest brothers are twins."

"What happened when you suggested she sleep with the others?"

Peter rubbed his hand over his face, and Ryan could see the toll this was taking on him. Peter had always been rather serious, but today his skin looked pale and unhealthy, his eyes were puffy, probably from lack of sleep, and his shoulders slumped forward in defeat.

"She demanded that I sign over the business and all of our assets to 'lie with my miscreant brothers.'" He used his fingers as quote marks indicating they were her derogatory words, not his.

Less than four hours ago, Ryan couldn't have imagined a woman so callous as to demand that sort of payment under the guise of love, but having met Jessie Evans, he now had a very clear picture. The woman was a first-class bitch.

Chapter Four

Ty lay on the bed, his wife cuddled to his side, his twin cuddled behind her, and his older brother asleep in the chair beside them. Mikayla had insisted that they needed to be together tonight, and Ty had wholeheartedly agreed. Of course, Peter wasn't going to climb onto the bed, but at least by having him this close, Mikayla had been able to fall asleep.

His eyes strayed to Peter's sleeping form. They'd managed to get all of their brothers into a conference call, and after the expected surprise, concern, and much arguing back and forth, they'd finally agreed to fight. Jessie Evans had no genuine claim over them, and to hand over their hard earned money without standing up for themselves just seemed wrong. Fortunately, Brock, Lachlan, Matt, Bryce, and John had managed to get the station pieced together and were able to lock up and travel back to Earth if it became necessary.

Ty really hoped it wasn't necessary.

A quick call to their lawyer had confirmed that a court date had been set for six days time. They'd been surprised by how quickly the system worked until their lawyer had explained that Jessie Evans's legal team had applied for the date nearly two years ago. The negotiations had just been part of the usual legal process under current laws. No case could go to court unless they could provide proof of failed negotiations.

Considering that Peter's lawyer was about to tell them to go to hell, Ty was fairly certain that would count as failed negotiations.

* * * *

The next afternoon Ryan ground his teeth as he listened to their lawyer explain what would happen next.

"As expected, her legal counsel was quite pleased that you didn't show up to the negotiating table." Their lawyer was a pleasant, middle-aged man with spectacles and thinning hair, and there was no doubt he knew his stuff. So far everything he'd predicted had come true. "Mrs. Davidson, they will definitely try to use your marriages as a way of proving Peter's intent. They may even drag up some personal details to try and paint you as a husband-stealing, gold-digging whore."

"Hey," Ryan protested, but their lawyer simply held up his hand.

"Get used to it," he said, shaking his head slowly. "These are the type of things that are liable to be said in court. If you react violently, the judge will kick you out of the courtroom and be less inclined to listen to your side of the story." He twisted his pen in his hand as if trying to find the exact words to get his point across. "If you seem to be upset, then the lawyers will use the offensive terms over and over in an effort to provoke you to violence and get you kicked out of the courtroom. Am I making myself clear? Their aim will be to get you to lose your temper. You need to stay very tightly in control."

The man took his glasses off, rubbed a finger over his left eye, and directed his attention to Mikayla. "I'm sorry, Mrs. Davidson, but this is liable to get very ugly, and you will likely cop the brunt of it. I want you and your husbands to be prepared for what you may encounter in court."

Mikayla nodded, obviously determined to stand up to the woman bold enough to sue her husbands, but every instinct Ryan owned screamed at him to remove his wife from the legal line of fire.

"Can we still make an offer?" Ty and Peter were obviously having the same thought process because they nodded in agreement to his question.

"That would be a very bad idea. Making an offer now would show weakness, and once the sharks smell blood in the water…"

"No," Mikayla said decisively, "I will not run and hide over a few nasty names. I know who I am, and I know why I married all of you."

She glanced around the room, daring any of them to dispute her right to make that decision. Their lawyer looked quite pleased.

"Excellent," he said. "I think it would be helpful if you were able to take the stand, perhaps explain the circumstances of your marriages. How you met them, why you decided to marry all of them not just one or t—"

"Hell, no," Ryan said as he turned to Mikayla. "Sweetheart, you don't have to do this. We'll just pay the money. I don't want you going through this."

Mikayla smiled so beautifully Ryan's heart hurt just thinking of her being savaged by Jessie Evans and her posse.

"It's not about the money," she said, touching his face with her fingertips. "It's about right and wrong. Peter did nothing wrong. We can't let her win like that."

"But I don't want you hurt," Ryan said as he pressed her hand harder against his face and closed his eyes.

"I won't be," she said, sounding very confident, "because I have my husbands beside me, and I know that they'll love me no matter what some nasty woman or her lawyers say."

Ryan nodded, wanting to say more, but also stunned by his sweet wife's conviction. She may have looked fragile, but she possessed a streak of courage a mile wide.

* * * *

Mikayla tried to sound very confident. She needed to fix this. Despite the fact that Jessie probably would've learned of Mikayla's marriage to the brothers eventually, she couldn't help but feel responsible for setting all of this in motion. If only she'd abided her husband's orders... She shook her head slightly. Nope, she couldn't even finish that thought. Following the orders of eight bossy husbands was a sure way to lose the person she believed herself to be.

It wasn't easy to hide the shaking in her fingers, but somehow she managed. She glanced at Ty and Peter's worried faces and forced herself to smile calmly. Going to court and standing up to this woman was the right thing to do, but a small worry niggled at the base of her skull. Despite everything she'd just told them about knowing they would love her no matter what, a small voice inside her whispered insidiously that maybe she was wrong.

Her husbands knew very little of her life before meeting them, and they knew absolutely nothing of her life before being abducted by people traffickers. They knew she had no family, but she'd always managed to avoid questions about her childhood. None of them even knew she'd been in the foster care system until the day she'd turned sixteen.

And not one of them knew what happened after that.

Their lawyer was still talking, and Mikayla tried to return her focus to the conversation.

"...we may well be able to convince the judge that Jessie Evans is actually the gold digger, but she plays the role of scorned lover quite well." Mikayla smiled, very pleased to hear that she wasn't the only one who could see past the woman's act. "But we need to be careful, or Peter will just be seen as a man who moved on to greener pastures with scant regard for the woman he'd promised to love."

He turned to Mikayla and held out his hand. "I will try to minimize the damage, but things will get a little rough. Let me know if you have any questions," he said as he shook her hand. "I'll see you in court on Thursday."

She nodded and followed him to the door. Once he'd gone, she turned to face her husbands. They all looked a little pale, and almost as one they started talking about her involvement in the court case. She held up her hand to silence them.

"Simple fact," she said very clearly. "Nasty things are going to be said about me whether I am there or not. At least this way I get to defend myself."

Ryan and Ty nodded thoughtfully, but Peter still looked miserable. Before he could apologize again, she moved into his arms and pressed a kiss to his lips. "First, I want a nap," she said on a yawn, "and then I want to go back to California for a couple of days." He nodded, pulled her closer, and turned toward the bedroom.

"Oh, no, not this time, brother," Ryan said as he followed them into the bedroom. "You can sleep in the chair if you want, but I want my wife in my arms. So you can either sleep on her other side or watch from a distance. Either way, Ty and I aren't going to be left out. Not today."

Surprisingly, Peter nodded, perhaps in resignation, and then climbed onto the bed and dragged Mikayla into the middle. He didn't look comfortable when Ryan slid onto the other side, or when Ty stretched out at the end of the bed and wrapped a hand around Mikayla's ankle, but Peter stayed there and held her as she fell asleep.

* * * *

Traveling back to California was a very good idea. Ty watched his wife talk animatedly to Tracey and her partners. Mikayla appeared relaxed, and it was certainly distracting her from the stress of the upcoming court date. As childish as it seemed, Ty was still hoping for a miracle so that he could spare his wife the pain and humiliation of having her life with them dissected and vilified.

Tracey laughed as her partners pulled her in for a tight hug. The four of them seemed very happy together. Rick, Tony and Ashton seemed very protective of Tracey in much the same way Ty and his brothers were toward Mikayla. They were also cops, and even though Ty worried for Tracey's well-being if her partners were hurt on duty, he also felt relieved that Tracey was well protected.

He shook his head minutely as he realized his faith in the human race had certainly been tainted by their experiences on the ice planet. Although, the realization didn't make him want to protect his wife any less.

"So have you set a date?" Mikayla asked in a very excited voice. He tuned in to the conversation hoping to catch on to whatever he'd missed.

"We're not planning anything over the top. Rick's parents and sister aren't pleased with their choice of lifestyle." Mikayla could tell by the way Tracey spat the words "choice" and "lifestyle" she was not thrilled by her soon-to-be in-laws' opinion. "And you know I have no family, so we thought we'd just have a civil ceremony with a couple of work colleagues and a few close friends." Tracey glanced up at Ty and then back to Mikayla. "When do you go home?"

By the beautiful, excited smile across Mikayla's face, Ty figured they weren't going home until after Tracey's wedding. And at the moment he couldn't think of anything more perfect than giving Mikayla a good memory of this trip to Earth.

He nodded when Tracey looked at him, and then the women giggled like teenagers and got down to the serious business of planning a wedding.

* * * *

"As you can see, Your Honor, Mr. Davidson and his brothers are all married to Miss Mikayla Noone. I offer these marriage certificates as evidence that clearly supports Ms. Evans's claim that her engagement to Mr. Peter Davidson also included his brothers." The bailiff handed the paperwork to the judge who looked through them without changing the expression on his face.

Jessie Evans had arrived at the courthouse wearing a simple, yet elegant and obviously expensive, summer dress. She was the picture of sweet innocence, and it made Peter want to strangle the woman. Obviously he'd given her far more ammunition than he'd realized.

It would've been difficult to sell the claim that Peter would fall for two such wildly different women, but by dressing in a similar fashion to Mikayla, Jessie had a much better chance.

How the hell had he missed Jessie's real personality? He'd once thought himself in love with the woman, but clearly the person she'd pretended to be was not the real person underneath. Peter clasped his hands together tightly, trying to still their shaking, as the judge turned to speak to Mikayla.

"Mrs. Davidson," he said in a kind voice. "Can you tell me the circumstances of your marriages? Where did you meet your husbands?"

She explained in a clear and concise voice exactly the circumstances of their first meeting, holding her head high as she explained about the human trafficking ring and her brief time spent in the world of prostitution. She left nothing out, and he couldn't have been more proud. Mikayla was one in a billion, and he'd thank every deity known to man for the rest of his life for bringing her to him.

Peter glanced at the woman he would've married and frowned at the malicious smile on her face. It was the only hint he'd seen that the woman wasn't quite as in control as she seemed. Surely the judge wouldn't consider that smile sweet.

"Why did you agree to marry all seven of the Davidson brothers?" the judge asked, seeming just a little perplexed that a woman could want so many husbands.

"Because I love them," she said simply. "And it's eight brothers. I met Bryce a few months after I married Lachlan, Brock, John, Matt, Peter, Ryan, and Ty in a civil ceremony the last time we were on Earth. My marriage to Bryce was filed, witnessed, and approved via intergalactic channels several months ago."

"Who the fuck is Bryce?" The woman's screech was so unexpected that Peter didn't even realize it was Jessie's voice until she jumped to her feet and screamed the question again. She looked like she intended to march up to where Mikayla sat and confront her nose to nose. Peter and his brothers were on their feet in an instant, but fortunately her lawyers and her father held her back. It didn't stop her from hurling obscenities. "Can't you tell the little whore is lying? Why would they even want that pathetic excuse for a woman as their wife? Let go of me!" she yelled at her father and pushed the man away. "She probably just gives them really good blow jobs."

"Ms. Evans!" the judge growled as he hit his gavel against the desk. "Counsel, control your client, or she will be removed from my courtroom."

The whole room had turned to watch Jessie throw her tantrum, but Peter's eye were only for his wife. She gave him a soft smile and sat serenely while the courtroom exploded in movement. He could hear Jessie's nasty words spewing from her mouth, but none of it meant a damn thing. Mikayla was his soul mate, his one true love, and he would cherish and protect her to his last breath.

* * * *

Mikayla couldn't quite believe the relief coursing through her. Some of the accusations that had been pointed her way had been completely hideous and very untrue, yet others had hit just a little too close to home. Living in such isolated circumstances, she really hadn't given much thought to how society would judge a woman with eight husbands. How ironic that the worst vitriol came from a woman wanting to steal seven of them from her.

She watched, surprised and maybe a little concerned for the woman and her mental health. The way she seemed to have completely lost her composure didn't quite seem normal.

Mikayla sat there, trying to look calm and composed but jumped in fright when the judge banged his wooden hammer against the desk and ordered Jessie be removed from the room.

When Jessie's frantic screeching finally faded down the hallway, the judge turned to Mikayla. "Mrs. Davidson, in light of the fact that Ms. Evans was obviously unaware of an eighth brother and, therefore, not as knowledgeable of the Davidson brothers as she claimed, I am dismissing her claim and finding in your favor. The court thanks you for your time." He smiled then said with a suspicious gleam in his eyes, "Go home to your husbands, Mrs. Davidson. It's obvious that they love you, and it's exactly where you belong."

She nodded as tears filled her eyes. She did belong to her men, and they belonged to her, and hopefully the past would leave them alone now to get on with their lives.

Chapter Five

Proposed Mining Planet M789zi.

Mikayla sighed as she entered the last report into the computer. Her satisfaction lasted all of two seconds before Ty dropped a heap more onto her desk. They'd been working their collective asses off since returning home three weeks ago. Tracey's wedding had been perfect, and she'd promised to contact Mikayla as soon as she returned from her honeymoon.

Tired but happy and relaxed for the first time in a long time, Mikayla put off starting the new pile of work and instead watched the newest specimen they'd collected. The cute little fur ball held a piece of vegetation between its paws as it munched away and watched her at the same time.

"What are you going to call it?"

Ty spared a glance at the cage and replied, "I'll need to do a complete genetic workup to be able to classify and name it correctly, but for the moment I'm calling it 'mouse.'"

Mikayla rolled her eyes. Men. He could've called it anything he wanted—they were the only ones on the planet for heaven's sake—but no, Ty had to call it a mouse. Plain, old, boring, little gray mouse! It may have looked a little like an Earth mouse, but it was far prettier. It had a cute elongated snout that twitched when food was near and luminous, expressive eyes that reminded her more of the marsupials in Australia back on Earth than common field mice. She watched it turn in a circle several times like a dog, and then it settled down for a nap.

"Why isn't it frightened of us?" They'd been told the largest creature on this planet was an insect, a teeny, tiny insect, not a mouse-like creature the size of a man's fist.

"I suspect that on this planet he's the 'king of the jungle,' so he's never needed to be frightened."

"Oh," Mikayla said, feeling a little stupid. She probably should've guessed that herself. The preliminary reports on this planet had discounted mammals—obviously incorrectly, judging by this cute little fur ball—reptiles, birds and pretty much all other life forms. Insects were scarce, though with so much plant life that would need insects for pollination it suggested they were not as scarce as they seemed.

"So what does this mean to the survey work and the contract in general?"

"Not sure yet," Ty said as he came to stand beside her. She wrapped her arms around his waist and rested her head on his chest as they both watched the furry little creature sleep. "We'll need to do a more intensive study of the local wildlife to determine how mining will affect them. Clearly the original survey was incomplete, and we can't really rely on any of the information provided, so we'll need to repeat that first." Ty pressed a kiss to the top of her head and pulled her closer. "Then when we get the geological survey results, we can determine whether the impact on the local environment can be minimized, whether the mineral ores are in sufficient quantities, or whether the proposed mining will need to be abandoned."

He pulled her closer and inhaled deeply. "You smell delicious." She giggled as he ran his tongue around the shell of her ear, but he groaned as he pulled away slightly. "If we didn't have so much work to do, Mrs. Davidson, I'd consider taking the afternoon off." She had no doubt on what an afternoon off with Ty would involve. She smiled as lots of sensual ideas ran through her mind.

Despite working side by side for most of the workday, Mikayla hadn't spent much down time with Ryan and Ty since they arrived home. They hadn't even gotten sweaty in the lab since that last time on the ice planet. Memories of the incredible orgasms they'd given her as they acted out their fantasy flooded through her brain, spreading heat to every inch of her body.

Ty sucked on her earlobe, and then nibbled his way to her lips. He kissed her, thrusting his tongue into her mouth, mimicking the ideas running through her head. He finally lifted away to draw a breath. "Hmmm, you taste delicious, too."

Ryan came into the lab looking rather harried. He smiled when he saw them pressed together but quickly broke up their fun.

"Sorry, Mikayla, but you two have about a million specimens to tag and identify, so unless you're planning a quickie against the wall, you're both out of luck."

Mikayla felt Ty's cock twitch against her hip and gasped when he rubbed himself against her. "What do you say?" he said with a suggestive leer. She laughed and went to move back to the counter where she'd been working. Ryan and Ty were always about the long, drawn-out—or as they called it—proper loving, so she was a little surprised at Ty's reluctance to let her go.

"You sure I can't talk you into being bad?" She laughed and swatted his hands away.

"Later," she promised, trying hard to ignore the arousal coursing through her veins.

* * * *

Ryan took a moment to study Ty's stiff movements. It was obvious that his brother was ready, willing, and able to not only please their wife but to do a very thorough job. At the beginning of a new contract, Ty was usually completely obsessive when they first landed on the planet. The man literally spent months barely sleeping and forgetting to eat while they explored their newest assignment. But this was the first time he'd had a wife to distract him.

Ryan watched his wife as she went back to entering reports into the lab's database and tried not to laugh at his brother's groan as he attempted to sit down with a hard-on. He'd been encouraging Ty for years to find some sort of balance between work and play, and Mikayla had managed to get him to do it just by being there. Ryan smiled at them both as images of what he and Ty would do with their beautiful wife when they had the chance invaded his mind. The woman was incredibly responsive to their every touch and gave the most incredible blow jobs. God, he felt the rush of blood to his groin as images of Mikayla on her knees taking his cock deep in her throat, his hands holding her still as he fucked her mouth over and over and over invaded his mind.

Shit. Ryan was half out of the chair before he realized what he was doing. It seemed Ty wasn't the only one being distracted by their beautiful wife today. Ryan discreetly adjusted his cock and tried to sit back down without groaning in pain.

A moment later he was out of the chair again. Damn. Sensual ideas invaded his every thought, and if he didn't find something to distract him, he was going to have Mikayla up against the wall in a matter of moments.

He left the lab to track down Peter. Technically, even though they didn't have an actual schedule, it was Peter's night with Mikayla. Considering the condition that both he and Ty seemed to be suffering, he felt it worth a quick chat with his older brother. Hell, the way he was feeling he'd be willing to beg and offer the man anything to swap nights with him and Ty.

He scrubbed a hand down his face feeling out of sorts. Hell, he hoped a full night of loving their wife together would help.

* * * *

Peter watched his brother's agitated movements and waited impatiently for him to speak. He still hadn't been able to rid himself of the guilt he felt for bringing Jessie Evans into their lives, and a part of him worried that Ryan was finally going to get around to saying something. Hell, Peter had called himself every fool name under the Earth's sun, surely it was his brother's turn.

Concern started to infiltrate his mind as Ryan didn't immediately start to speak. Ryan was usually clowning around, so it was quite a rarity to see the man lost for words. But Peter couldn't force any words past his tightening throat either.

"We need her," Ryan finally blurted out.

Peter nodded carefully. He knew Ryan and Ty needed help in the lab at this stage of their contract. They always did, but they already had Mikayla helping them, so he wasn't sure what Ryan meant by "needing her." Confused for a moment, Ryan's meaning finally became clear when the man adjusted the rigid length of his cock to a more comfortable position in his jeans. Judging by the pained expression on Ryan's face, it wasn't comfortable enough.

"You're talking about tonight?" Peter asked. Ryan nodded quickly. "Sure, I've got a heap of work to do anyway, but whatever you two are planning, don't play too rough. Mikayla spent last night in Brock's bed, and judging by some of the sounds, I think Brock has some new toys." He shook his head as he laughed at his observation. "Those two have been going at it like bunnies for the last few months. I guess Mikayla likes his new toys. Lucky he didn't come on holidays with us, or we mightn't have gotten any time with her." Peter knew he was babbling, but the silly relief of not having to listen to his brother's criticism, no matter how well-deserved, was making him a bit giddy.

Ryan nodded stiffly and left the room, leaving Peter to wonder if he was the reason for his brother's out of character behavior or not.

* * * *

For the rest of the afternoon, Ty struggled to concentrate on his work. Discovering and identifying new animal and insect species had always been his favorite part of a new planet, but this time it just didn't seem to hold his interest. Over and over his gaze strayed to the woman working on the computer beside him. Mikayla glanced up and caught him staring once more.

Geez, it was almost like he was a randy teenager again. Sex seemed to be about the only thing in his mind.

"Ty? Everything okay?" Her soft, sweet voice full of concern did absolutely nothing to deflate the painful hard-on threatening to burst open his pants.

"Uh, sure," he managed to mumble and then turned back to the specimen he'd been trying to classify. He could feel his face burning with embarrassment. What the hell was wrong with him?

He could sense her studying him, trying to understand his unusual behavior, but he didn't really have an explanation for his condition. Regressing back to his teenage years was not something he wanted to admit out loud. He was so busy trying to convince himself that it was just imagination that he didn't hear Mikayla move until she touched his elbow.

And then he was lost.

"I need you," he whispered as he hauled her onto his lap, lifted her dress over her head, and swept her underwear to her ankles. She smiled and helped to undo his way-too-tight jeans and then moved to straddle him. He thrust into her quickly, ramming his cock to the hilt without pause. She gasped and moaned at the abrupt intrusion but didn't pull away. Mindless with need, he lifted her and dragged her back onto his cock, his hips tilting to take her deeper with every thrust. Already he could feel his climax nearing, and he swallowed, trying to slow himself down, trying to remember Mikayla's pleasure as well as his own.

Unable to reach her clit in this position, he pushed a dry finger straight into her ass, wiggling the digit as her pussy began to cream around his cock. Her orgasm hit her just as his began, his dick pulsing, throbbing, shooting his seed deep into her body.

She fell forward, completely spent, as he held her close and worried at his own loss of control. Never before had he taken a woman without seeing to her pleasure first. Only his wife's amazing responsiveness saved him from being the kind of asshole lover he despised.

"Damn it, Ty!" Ryan's voice sounded angry, hurt, and amazingly breathless. Before Ty or Mikayla could react, Ryan had lifted Mikayla off Ty's lap, pressed her up against the wall, and driven his cock deep into her slick flesh. Just like Ty, Ryan set a ridiculous, frantic pace. Realizing that his brother was beyond reason, Ty moved to hold Mikayla in his arms, cushioning her as his brother fucked her. She moaned in delight at the new angle, and Ryan was able to press against her clit. She screamed as she exploded in orgasm, Ryan right behind her. Both of them grunted with the final thrust and then stilled.

All three of them breathed heavily for several moments before Ryan pulled away, slowly extricating himself and helping Mikayla to her feet. She wobbled with exhaustion, and Ty wrapped his arms around her so that she wouldn't fall.

"Come on, darlin'," he said in what he hoped was a soothing voice. "Let's get cleaned up." She nodded tiredly and let him lift her into his arms. She was completely exhausted, and by the time he got her to the shower, he understood why. Faded pink stripes covered her ass and thighs, and if Ty were to guess, he'd say they'd been done by a leather belt of sorts. The lines were very straight and uniform, so it was obvious that Brock knew what he was doing.

Ty traced the faded pink line and asked curiously, "Did this hurt?"

Mikayla turned and smiled reassuringly. "Yes," she said with a wink, "but in a very good way."

"Maybe one day I could watch." He wasn't even sure why he'd said that. He'd never been interested in bondage or pain for pleasure, but his wife's beatific smile had him salivating for it. His cock grew again and he groaned as need pulsed through him once more. "Maybe you should get some rest," he said to Mikayla as he backed away from the shower. He had intended to climb in with her, but considering his state of mind, it could be a very, very long shower.

Mikayla looked at him with a raised eyebrow, obviously picking up his strange mood swings. "I'm fine," she said slowly. "But maybe you have a different reason for me to stay out of the lab?" She held his gaze, daring him to be dishonest. When he didn't immediately answer, she crossed her arms and waited.

Embarrassed that he would even consider lying to his wife over something so trivial, Ty nodded and smiled. "It would seem that Ryan and I are both very distracted by our lovely wife today. We have plans for you, Mrs. Davidson, so maybe you should get some rest while you can."

She looked a little concerned, and he wanted nothing more than to step into the shower and pull her into his embrace. But, considering his cock was pressed hard up against his jeans again, he knew exactly where that would lead. So he took a step back and tried to smile reassuringly.

She smiled back but couldn't hide the concern in her eyes. Feeling his control slipping once more, he nodded and left the room before he could do anything stupid.

* * * *

Mikayla washed herself down as worry wiggled through her brain. Ryan and Ty had stopped treating her like something fragile long before any of the others, but their behavior today was definitely out of character for both of them.

Did they regret fucking her in the lab? The sex had been raw and aggressive and a stamping of ownership, rather than the playful lovemaking they'd resorted to recently. She'd loved every moment of what happened in the lab, but it was the aftermath that had her troubled.

By the time she got out of the shower, she was feeling more tired than she'd thought she should be, but considering what happened last night, maybe it wasn't so surprising. Her session with Brock had left her completely sated, and she'd slept well, but if Ryan and Ty were serious, she was in for a long night. When those two started playing with her, the lovemaking could go on for hours. Maybe she should get some sleep while she had the chance.

She crawled naked into Ryan's bed, pulled the sheet up to her shoulders and curled up for a quick nap.

She woke to a warm arm around her middle and a thick cock pressed against her ass. Mikayla opened her eyes to find Ryan lying in front of her. Ty pulled her closer, kissing the back of her neck and rubbing his hard cock against her butt cheeks. Ryan leaned in to kiss her softly, but the heat quickly caught them both, and he began kissing her deeply, frantically. She moved against him, writhing between the brothers as her arousal grew.

Thick fingers found her clit, pressing and massaging the needy button until she was crying out for their possession. Cold lube made her gasp, but Ty quickly worked it into her back passage, setting every nerve ending alight.

Ryan lifted her leg, pressed his cock against her pussy, and entered her in one smooth thrust. Mikayla saw the strained look on his face as he controlled his entry and reined in his need, so she smiled reassuringly. Ty spread her ass cheeks, placed his cock against her anus, and hurriedly pushed his way into her tight back passage.

Together they held still, letting her adjust, kissing and caressing her soothingly. As heat built, they started moving slowly, carefully, one sliding in as the other slid out, over and over until she was moaning with pleasure. She could feel them both trying to hold back, trying to control their lust, but then, like a dam breaking, they suddenly got more forceful, needier, thrusting deeper, harder. Their breathing harsh, their grunts animalistic. Fingers, she didn't know whose, found her clit and squeezed hard. She screamed as orgasm crashed over her, and her men started pounding into her ass and pussy at the same time.

The intensity overwhelmed her. They came in unison, filling her body with their seed, grunting their release, whispering their love.

Finally, exhausted and replete, all three lay collapsed on the mattress, still joined, still wrapped in each other's arms, but Mikayla was so exhausted that sleep claimed her quickly.

* * * *

"What the hell was that?" Ty whispered irritably. It seemed easier to yell at his brother than to accept his part in the whole mess. Ryan shook his head, obviously feeling as annoyed as Ty. Never had they lost control like that. Double penetration took practice and finesse. They were always aware that Mikayla could be injured if they didn't show some restraint, but today neither of them seemed in control of their libido.

Thank god Mikayla had fallen asleep with a smile on her face. If she'd been hurt or upset, he would never have forgiven himself.

"I think…" Ryan took a deep breath and tried again. "I think maybe we should get off the base for a few days. Let Mikayla have some time with the others."

Ty nodded. Whatever the hell was going on with his hormones seemed to be affecting his brother as well. At least if they were off base, they couldn't accidentally injure the woman they loved. And the time away might also give them a chance to understand this desperate need to claim the woman who already belonged to them.

Chapter Six

What the fuck?

Peter stood in the empty lab and looked around irritably. It seemed that both of his youngest brothers had decided to goof off again. Despite the fact that Ryan and Ty were qualified veterinarians and research scientists with a very important function within their family business, somehow they still managed to act like a couple of teenagers at times. Granted, it wasn't usually this early in their contract, but then they hadn't had a wife to play with before.

Peter was about to go find them and tear a strip or two from their hides when the cage with the small little mouse-like creature caught his attention. The tiny animal had some sort of liquid coming from its eyes that looked a lot like tears. It was currently rubbing the fluid all over its fur. Curious. Was the creature ill, or was it some sort of grooming habit? Now if he just had a veterinarian to ask.

Damn it! Peter spun from the room as his anger spiked. He'd already told Ryan that he and Ty could swap his night with Mikayla. God help them if he found them in bed with their wife. As much as they all loved the woman, they still had a business to run.

Peter stomped down the hallway, images of what Ryan and Ty and Mikayla were probably up to fueling his anger. Memories of the first time he'd seen Mikayla orgasm skipped through his mind. She'd been facedown over a bench in the lab as Matt finger fucked her pussy and ass and explained all the dark needs of each brother. He hadn't been lying. Peter loved to take a woman from behind, just bend her over and plough into her heat again and again until they were both screaming in orgasm. But, so far, he'd managed to control his darker needs with Mikayla. She was his wife, and he loved and respected her and would always be the gentle lover her other husbands weren't.

He growled low in his throat as his cock lengthened and throbbed in his pants. Great. Mikayla was currently being fucked by two irresponsible husbands, and he was left standing in the middle of the hallway with the mother of all hard-ons.

He ran into Ryan and Ty as he turned the next corner. His fist connected with Ryan's jaw without him having given the action any real thought. Surprised at his own behavior Peter took a step back.

"Peter? What the fuck?" Ryan clenched his hands and looked angry enough to tear him to shreds. Ty looked ready to help him.

"I said you could sleep with her tonight, not fuck her all afternoon." Peter wasn't even sure where the words were coming from. He just knew if he didn't get them out, he was going to throw more punches.

Ryan dropped his fists and took a step back.

"We're sorry," he said in a defeated tone. "Look we're...um...going to collect some more specimens. You know... Maybe climb the mountain to the west and see if we can find any other signs of life that the first team missed."

Peter nodded carefully, still trying to rein in his anger. What the hell was wrong with him? He didn't get jealous. Hell, he'd given up his engagement to Jessie because she hadn't been willing to sleep with his brothers. Sharing Mikayla with them was like a dream come true. And having Jessie out of their lives was a godsend. He shuddered at the very thought of life with that woman.

"Report in twice a day," he said even though he knew his youngest brothers knew the protocol better than he did. "Stay safe," he managed to force past his numb lips before he turned stiffly to go back to his own office.

By the time he made it back to his workspace, he was sweating from the strain of his hard cock against his pants. He flicked the lock on the door, undid his jeans with a grateful sigh, and stroked the turgid flesh soothingly.

Every cell in his body demanded that he find Mikayla and slake his lust, but a small amount of sanity held him back. Whatever had happened with Ryan and Ty would've left her exhausted and, knowing those two miscreants, maybe even a little raw. He couldn't imagine her wanting another cock fucking her right now.

Images of what he wanted to do danced through his imagination as he stroked his cock more rapidly. A moment later his orgasm burst from him. Pearly white seed coated his hand and splashed onto his pants as his climax went on and on. He leaned his head back on the headrest for a moment as he tried to calm down. Shaking, breathing heavily, Peter finally grabbed a cloth, cleaned himself up and then tried to tuck his already recovering cock into his pants.

But images of fucking Mikayla from behind, claiming her aggressively, marking her with his cum, filled his head again.

What the hell was wrong with him?

* * * *

Dinner was a strange affair. Ryan and Ty had taken off on a specimen gathering hike, apparently having found their unexpected, unplanned excursion absolutely urgent, and Peter kept looking at her with an equal amount of lust and worry in his eyes. Lachlan was still keeping his distance, and John, Matt, and Bryce seemed unusually subdued.

Only Brock seemed to be his normal self, but when he joked about spanking Mikayla's ass, Peter looked like he was going to strip the flesh from Brock's hide. She hadn't even gotten around to asking Peter why his knuckles were swollen and seemed to be bruised.

With the awkward meal finally done, Mikayla stood to collect the plates expecting Peter to join her like he usually did. But tonight he seemed completely out of sorts because he grabbed her hand and placed the dishes back on the table.

"The others are capable of washing the dishes, aren't you, brothers?" They all looked at Peter like he'd grown a second head—the dishes had been Mikayla and Peter's sacred nightly ritual ever since they'd met—but all of the men nodded their agreement. A moment later, tucked tightly against Peter's side, Mikayla found herself walking quickly toward Peter's living quarters.

As soon as he had the door closed, he lifted her dress over her head and discarded it carelessly. He dropped to his knees, pulled her panties down, and pressed his marauding tongue against her clit a moment later. Weak at the knees, Mikayla almost fell on her ass, but strong hands held her pressed against his face. Licking, sucking, nibbling, Peter worried her clit until she was gasping, on the verge of orgasm, ready to explode.

He stood, his eyes looking wild. He pulled her against his chest, and shook as he spoke words she'd never expected to hear from him. "Tell me to get out. I want you too much. Tell me to leave, so I don't hurt you."

Shivering with her own need, Mikayla wrapped her arms around him and held on tight. "I love you," she said, hoping he understood just how much those three little words meant, "and I know you'd never hurt me." She pulled back and looked up to his handsome face. "And besides," she said, rubbing her aching clit against his hard erection, "I'm not fragile."

"You don't understand," he said, taking deep, gulping breaths as if his control held by a thread. "What Matt said that day in the lab, about our darker desires"—she nodded—"he wasn't exaggerating. I…I like to take a woman from behind. Oh god, Mikayla, I need you."

She smiled, pulled from his arms, and crawled onto the end of the bed, her ass in the air as clear invitation. Peter's movement was explosive. He dragged his pants to his knees, grabbed her hips, and thrust into her in one hard shove. He slammed into her over and over, his fingers digging into her soft flesh as he pounded her. Thrilled, gasping for air, practically purring from his violent possession, she screamed when he slapped her thigh.

It didn't hurt, but it was so unexpected coming from this man that she tipped over into orgasm. Her pussy milked his cock as he plundered her soft flesh. Harder and deeper, stronger until he growled and held still. She could feel his cock pulsing as he pumped his seed deep into her womb.

He fell forward onto her, pressing her face down into the mattress, his weight cutting off her air for a moment, until he rolled to the side and pulled her with him. She could feel his cock slowly softening as her pussy pulsed with aftershocks.

"I'm sorry," he said very quietly. Tears filmed her vision at the anguish in his voice.

"Why?" she asked, trying to hide her own disquiet.

"I promised myself that I'd never get rough with you. That I would love you and worship you for the rest of our lives, and I just broke that promise."

"Peter," she said as she tried to roll over, but he held her still. She lay in his arms for a moment wondering what to say to alleviate his guilt. Because it was obviously guilt driving him at this moment. "I didn't ask you to make that promise," she whispered finally.

"But I wanted to honor you as my wife not take you like a common whore." She didn't know whether to laugh or cry. Taken the wrong way that could be considered an insult. She tried to roll over again to face him, and after a moment's resistance he let her.

Touching his face softly, she said, "Peter, I love that you love me enough to lose control. You didn't hurt me, in fact I loved every moment, so please stop beating yourself up. I love you. Everything about you. The gentle, the rough, the wild, I'll take it all and love you forever."

He looked slightly relieved by her little speech, but he still had a haunted look in his eyes. Hopefully, time would prove to him that she was serious. He leaned forward, kissed her gently, and gave her a goofy grin. "Can I make love to you properly now?"

She smiled at the touch of humor. "Of course."

Hours later every muscle and bone in Mikayla's body felt melted and pliant, and she fell into a deep sleep beside her husband.

* * * *

Mikayla wandered through the empty lab wondering what on Earth to do next. She'd finished inputting all of Ryan and Ty's notes into the computer, but with them still out collecting samples, there was no more work coming in.

She checked that the live specimens were properly housed, watered, and fed, watched the little furry critter clean itself for a few minutes, and finally sat back in her chair. She supposed that she could go see if John or Matt had some filing they needed done, or maybe get an early start on dinner, but she felt restless without Ryan and Ty here.

She still didn't understand their sudden withdrawal. It had literally taken months after her miscarriage for them to return to the energetic, athletic, and demanding lovers she'd known, but now, after some of the most incredible sex the three of them had shared, Ryan and Ty had disappeared from her life completely. Mikayla growled silently at her own overdramatization of the problem, but it really did feel like they were gone for good. They hadn't even said good-bye.

"Ah, there you are," John said happily as he entered the lab. "I've got a spare afternoon as soon as I feed and water the critters."

"Already done," she said, taking his hand and showing him the various cages and their unusual inhabitants.

"Well then," he said with a brilliant smile. "Would you care to join me for a stroll in the gardens?" He held his elbow out for her to take, and she laughed at his impersonation of a proper gentleman. He was the one who'd taught her how to suck cock, so she knew he was anything but.

"Why certainly, kind sir," she managed to say between giggles.

The garden was really just a small clearing that was still part of the research facility's compound, but it was full of interesting plants and strange colored flowers that practically defied description. The preliminary reports had identified that most of the plant life on this planet was poisonous and, therefore, explained the lack of animal life. Considering what they'd found so far, it seemed a poorly researched idea.

As they walked further, Mikayla noticed that John didn't seem to be walking quite so naturally as he'd been before. A quick glance at his crotch answered the question as to why. She stepped in front of him, stopping his forward momentum with a hand over his hard erection.

"Is there something I can help you with?" she asked with a wide grin on her face. John returned her grin, but his eyes had the same wild look as Peter's had last night. John nodded frantically and pushed her to her knees. Without pause he ripped open his pants, grabbed his cock, and shoved it into her mouth. Surprised by his rough entry she gagged as he hit the back of her throat. The sound seemed to settle something inside him because he pulled out and then slid back in slowly. Carefully he built the rhythm, his hands shaking in her hair as he obviously held himself back. Mikayla moved to brace one hand against his thigh and wrap the other around his balls. He'd always warned her he could get pretty rough, but until this moment she hadn't really believed him.

"Good girl," he said shakily as she gripped his balls tighter. He held her still as he fucked her face, sweat pouring down his abdomen and thighs as he seemed to strain to hold on to his sanity. A moment later his movement faltered, lost rhythm, pushed deep and held as his cum poured into her throat. She swallowed frantically to keep up, licking and sucking him clean and then managing to caress his softening cock with her tongue the way he liked.

Finally she unwrapped her stiff fingers from around his balls. She'd been concentrating so hard on not hurting him accidentally that her hand cramped as she removed her grip. He saw her predicament and helped her to stand as he kissed each finger on her sore hand.

"Are you okay, princess?"

"Yes," she said with a smile. When he grabbed for her dress, she moved out of his range. He raised his eyebrow in silent question. "I...um...I'm good." When he frowned, she realized he wouldn't let up until he had the full answer. "Yesterday was kind of intense. Between Ryan and Ty and Peter, I don't think I need another orgasm for a while." John still didn't look convinced but he nodded.

"Did they hurt you?" He looked quite angry at the thought, and she moved into his arms quickly to reassure him.

"No. None of you have ever hurt me. Not ever. And none of you have done anything that I wasn't happy for you to do. Are you listening to me, John? I'm just a little worn out, but nobody did anything to hurt me."

He nodded stiffly and she leaned up to press a kiss against the underside of his jaw. Desperate to placate his anger at his brothers she tried to inject a little humor. "And besides, that's one you owe me. Next time I need an orgasm, I'll be ordering you to your knees." He laughed softly and hugged her harder.

"I'm looking forward to it."

* * * *

Lachlan came into the kitchen while she was cooking dinner. She felt a strange type of relief when she saw him. Peter and John and Ryan and Ty had all been acting out of character, so she was a little relieved to see the brother who wasn't sleeping with her at the moment.

"You look tired, little one," he said by way of greeting.

She nodded warily. The one and only time she'd been sick since meeting her husbands, Lachlan had basically taken over her life. He hadn't let her eat, drink, shower, or sleep alone until he was convinced that she was one hundred percent well again. She almost giggled out loud at the memory. He'd been very sweet, but once she'd started to feel better, his overprotectiveness had begun to chafe.

Ironically, a little TLC wouldn't go astray at the moment, especially if it *wasn't* coupled with wild sex. She'd had more than enough of that for the moment.

"Can I help with anything?"

"I'm nearly done," she said confidently, "but I'd love a foot rub in a few minutes."

Lachlan smiled at her request, perhaps even a little relieved that she wasn't trying to goad him into spanking her like she'd done for the last few months. They hadn't made love since before her miscarriage, but even though his physical withdrawal hurt, she felt emotionally closer to him now than she ever had. Overall, it had been a good thing for them to step back from the sexual side of their Dom/sub relationship for a while and get to know each other better.

She finished the vegetables, checked the roast, and then sat sideways on the kitchen stool beside Lachlan. She leaned against the wall as he lifted her feet onto his lap and gave her another of his heavenly foot rubs. The man really was a master at massage.

"When will Ryan and Ty be back?" she asked. Lachlan continued to knead the ball of her foot as he glanced up to her face.

"I'm not really sure. The trip wasn't exactly planned, but they've checked in twice today, so they're all right." He looked at her thoughtfully for a moment, perhaps debating whether to ask his question. "Do you know why they left the way they did?"

She shook her head. "Not really, but it was right after sharing me. They got a little rougher than usual, but nothing bad happened. They didn't hurt me or anything."

"I was talking to John, and he was worried he got a little rough with you, too." She didn't want to nod a yes, but she couldn't really lie. Lachlan saw the answer in her eyes because he nodded as if she'd said yes. "Peter doesn't seem to be himself either."

Lachlan just waited for her reaction to that statement before he pulled her onto his lap and held her close.

"I'd say there was something in the water," she half-heartedly joked, "but we brought the water with us."

"What about the others?"

She shook her head against his chest. "They've been normal. Honestly, the sex has been wonderful—maybe a little too abundant—but definitely good. It's been their reactions afterward that are concerning. Ryan and Ty took off on an unplanned excursion, Peter has been moping around all day, and John went and ratted himself out to his big brother."

She felt Lachlan's chest rumble with laughter. It did sound a little funny when she said it that way, but it was essentially what John had done. Half of her men were acting weirdly, and it would be really nice to understand why.

"Could there be something in the water?" she asked, feeling just a little freaked. If they all started pulling away she'd be even more alone than when she'd miscarried. At least back then she'd had Bryce to hold her. Lachlan must've felt the shiver of apprehension that worked its way down her spine because he pulled her closer and ran a soothing hand through her hair.

"Probably not the water, but I'm beginning to suspect that something Ryan, Ty, Peter, and John were exposed to is affecting them somehow. Maybe something increasing their libido or overriding the control center in their brains." He was quiet for a moment then lifted her off his lap and placed her on her feet. "Sorry, little one, but I need to talk to Matt. With his background in pathology he might be able to identify something with a few blood tests. I'm sure Peter and John would be happy to hand over some blood if it meant finding out what's going on."

Mikayla nodded and stepped back to the oven to check her roast once more. Lachlan was almost out the door but turned back quickly to give her one more instruction. "If any of your husbands come on too strong, use that earsplitting whistle Ryan taught you, and I'll come intervene."

She rolled her eyes, certain that even affected by some unknown chemical, her husbands would cut off their favorite body parts before ever hurting her. Mischief gripped her and she couldn't help but ask the obvious question. "And what if that husband is you?"

Lachlan assessed her for a moment and then said confidently, "It won't be."

He left the room before she could come up with a smart-ass answer. Unfortunately, even though she knew it was meant as a reassurance, she couldn't quite shake off the thought that he'd managed to resist her for a couple of months, so chemical or no, he'd had plenty of practice.

She decided to make dessert as well, anything to keep her hands busy and hold the tears at bay. Damn.

Chapter Seven

"We can't go back to the lab in this state." Ryan rolled his eyes at his brother, the master of the understatement. They'd left Mikayla behind in the hopes of getting their libidos under control, and things just seemed to have gotten worse. They'd only been away from the base for one night, yet he'd had more wet dreams than he could remember even from his teenage years. He was almost convinced that if he masturbated one more time he was going to rub the top layer of skin off his cock.

"So what do we do?" he asked Ty. He felt completely exasperated, but heading back to the lab and Mikayla just didn't sound like a very good idea. Ty shook his head, obviously having no answer to his question.

"Do you think the others are affected as well?" Ryan felt his blood run hot and cold at Ty's softly spoken question. What if the others were walking penises as well? Ryan sure felt like his cock was doing the thinking for him.

"I don't know," he said, trying to hold the fear for Mikayla in check. At the moment he and Ty probably presented more of a problem than any of the others. He couldn't imagine Lachlan or Brock or even Matt not contacting them if they had such a serious problem. "But maybe we should call in. Explain to Matt. See if he can find a reason for what's happening."

Ty nodded and reached for the communication equipment.

* * * *

John looked as relieved as Peter felt. It was childish and pathetic, but he was really glad he wasn't the only one affected by whatever was going on. Matt led them both into the lab, gathered the stuff he would need to take blood samples, and set to work.

Once he'd collected and labeled their samples, he grabbed a new needle and turned it on himself. He cursed a blue streak as he tried to collect his own blood. It took Peter a few moments to realize that Matt's hands were now shaking. He'd been fine when they wandered into the lab.

"It's in the lab?" Peter asked Matt. John made a noise of surprise, but Matt seemed to be gritting his teeth as he nodded.

"Buzz Lachlan. Tell him to keep everyone out of the lab. Until we know what's affecting us, no one else comes in. Are we clear?" Peter nodded and headed over to the intercom system. He hesitated when John asked, "If whatever is affecting us is in here, wouldn't it be better to leave?"

"Maybe," Matt said slowly. "When was the last time you were in the lab?"

"Yesterday," John answered quickly.

"And do you feel like its effect lessened over time?"

Peter glanced at John and then shrugged his shoulders. "Maybe a little."

"Did you feel it spike when we walked in earlier?"

"Yes," John answered, "but I was thinking of Mikayla." Peter nodded in agreement. He, too, had been thinking of their lovely wife, a subject he'd had on his mind a lot the last day or so.

"Okay, whatever is doing this is A, in the room, B, has lasting effects that maybe reduce slowly over time, and C, seems to reinfect with additional exposure. My best chance is to stay here in the lab, test everything, and try to match it back to whatever contaminants we find in our blood work." Matt ran his hands down his face, clearly feeling overwhelmed. "Assuming of course that it actually shows up in our blood work," he added.

"We should stay here as well, help however we can. It might be enough to distract us so that we're not tempted to seek out Mikayla," John said quietly. Peter heartily agreed. There was no way to tell how Mikayla would cope if all eight of her husbands suddenly became animals only interested in sex.

"Shit," Matt said as he undid the top button of his jeans. "You've coped with this for how long? I'm ready to go insane, and it's only been a few minutes."

"It wasn't this bad before. It's like it multiplied tenfold. Tell us what to do," Peter demanded as he tried to ignore the throbbing in his own groin. "What are we looking for? What are the most likely sources?"

Matt shook his head as if trying to clear it. "On an alien planet it could be practically anything."

"What would it be on Earth? It's a type of aphrodisiac, right?"

"Seems to be," Matt agreed in a strangled voice. "Something airborne, maybe an animal pheromone or scent? We're certainly reacting like dogs to a female in heat."

The intercom buzzed before Peter actually got around to calling Lachlan. Fortunately, it was Lachlan.

"I've just heard from Ryan and Ty," he said without preamble. "They're both affected, even more so outside the compound. Have you been able to get the blood tests started?"

"Not exactly," Matt said, still sounding like he was clenching his teeth, "but I'm fairly certain that something in the lab is causing the problem. It's affecting me now as well. Almost the moment I walked in the room my heart rate and blood pressure shot up, and well, I seem to be suffering the same symptoms." He dropped his hand over his hard cock but seemed to realize what he was doing and deliberately pulled back.

Peter glanced down to realize he was doing the same thing. He ripped his hand away and tried to think clearly.

"Do Ryan and Ty have any theories?"

"Only that it seems to be worse outside the compound," Lachlan replied.

"What about you, Matt?" Lachlan asked, but before Matt could answer, a memory popped into Peter's mind, and he moved quickly to interrupt the conversation.

"Lachlan, I remember reading something about a study on mouse tears back on Earth. There was research that suggested that the male's tears were an aphrodisiac to the female. When I was in here the other day, the gray mouse-like critter we've got in the lab had some sort of fluid leaking from its eyes and was rubbing it all over its body. Could it be mating season for these things? Would another animal's mating musk affect humans?"

They moved closer to the little critter's cage and watched as the little ball of fluff groomed itself and smoothed its tears all over its body. The damn thing was practically shining with so much fluid covering its fur.

"Hell, it's a solid theory," Matt said with an awkward shrug as he once again adjusted his cock.

"I'll get onto Ryan and Ty. See if they have any objections to dropping our furry visitor back into the wild."

Matt, John and Peter waited in tense silence until Lachlan's voice came through the intercom. "Okay, Ryan says releasing the creature will at least give as an idea if the effect is lessened over time— assuming that the critter is causing the problem. If nothing else it will eliminate one possible cause and we can go onto the next. Make sure you release it outside the compound. The last thing we need is one of these things crawling back into our quarters."

Matt nodded at his brothers then moved to grab the cage containing the mouse-like creature. Peter moved closer to the intercom. "Lachlan, keep Mikayla safe. Don't let any of us near her."

"Understood."

* * * *

Matt tried to walk a straight line with his eyes damn near crossed and his cock so hard it practically had a personality of its own. He walked out the gate and several hundred yards into the brush land before opening the cage door and letting their former guest leave.

What happened next was a little disconcerting. Several gray furry bodies came running from different directions, all landing near what Matt was beginning to suspect was a female. Some of the newcomers fought amongst themselves, others tried to mount the tiny creature. They were wild and aggressive, and the female seemed to thoroughly enjoy it.

She made a loud purring sound as she rubbed her eyes and then smoothed her paws all over her furry body. The noise and mating musk seemed to drive the males into a frenzy. And damn it all to hell, Matt could feel his own erection getting harder. How was that even possible?

But it did lend credence to Peter's theory.

Spinning on his heel, Matt practically sprinted back to the compound and locked himself back in the lab with Peter and John. He headed straight for the intercom.

"Lachlan, I think we have a fairly solid theory. It looks like it is mating season for those creatures. Maybe Ryan and Ty should head back to the compound, avoiding every critter on this damn planet, and we'll see if we can lessen the effect with medication or vitamins or something." He glanced at his brothers, relieved to see their faces less strained. He realized then that, even though he still felt incredibly horny, and his cock still had a mind of its own, he wasn't quite as frantic as he'd been around the furry creature. "We need to contact a couple of medical researchers and see if they can find a permanent solution. Hopefully it's only a seasonal thing, but this is going to affect mining operations rather severely. I don't even want to think about what could happen in a mining colony affected by mating musk. Hell, we thought the last planet was fucked up."

"I'll get onto it right now," Lachlan assured him. "Good job, guys."

Matt looked over at Peter to see the man smiling. "What's so funny?" he asked, feeling his irritation spike unreasonably. Thank god Mikayla wasn't here because he had an awful feeling he'd be fighting his brothers for the right to mount their wife. Shit.

"I was just thinking," Peter said, his voice sounding like he held back laughter, "that we've just discovered the first women's perfume that can overcome erectile dysfunction."

Matt started to laugh, Peter and John joining him a moment later. Hell, the medical possibilities were enormous, and there was a really good chance that they would far outweigh the possible profits from mining. Maybe their contract on this planet would be done early.

* * * *

Mikayla sat on the sofa flanked by Bryce and Brock. It felt a little over the top, but considering that her *musk-affected* husbands now outnumbered the *not-musk-affected* husbands, she could understand the inclination. She just hoped this didn't convince them all to tiptoe around her again.

"How much longer?" she asked, trying to sound like she wasn't whining. She'd been sitting around for two whole days. Having nothing to do was starting to piss her off. At least in the lab she would have computer work and filing to do. She hadn't even been allowed to cook the evening meals.

"Baby girl," Brock said in his warning voice that usually preceded an O-ring gag, "you need to be patient."

"Fuck patient," she said very deliberately. Hell, if he made her wear the gag, at least it might lead to something more interesting than sitting around and staring at the ceiling. Brock grinned, obviously well aware of her intentions, and then went back to reading his book. Damn, he was a really good Dom.

She growled in annoyance. Bryce chuckled at her pathetic tantrum but pulled her onto his lap and held her tight. He didn't, however, let her wriggle against his cock. Damn. Maybe the mating musk had affected her, too. She certainly felt ready to mate with all her men.

"I just got a communication from the medical research labs," Lachlan said as he walked through the door. "They're sending three scientists to continue the work Matt has begun. All of them are women which I think is a damn good idea considering what the musk does to men. They should be here in a couple of days."

Mikayla was on her feet as anger surged through her.

"Did you just say that three women are coming to the same facility that is not only my home," she growled as she started pacing back and forth, "but also happens to contain five of my husbands affected by the need to mate?"

Lachlan's smile was *so not helping* her temper.

"Baby girl," Brock said again, this time more forcefully. She'd just about had it. Dom or not, husband or not, trying to protect her or not, she wasn't putting up with anymore condescending bullshit. If she wanted to be angry about other women moving in on her men, then she had the right to be fucking angry.

Bryce seemed to be holding back a laugh, but Lachlan's next comment had her rounding on him in anger.

"It would seem, little one, that the men are not the only ones to be affected by the mating musk." She really, really wanted to hit him about now, but the fact that she'd have to jump just to reach his smug face and that she'd probably break a bone in her hand against his chiseled jaw, held her back.

Oh, yeah, and the fact that violence was wrong.

And he was her husband, and she loved him.

What the fuck was wrong with her?

Chapter Eight

Ty looked up as Lachlan entered the room with Mikayla draped over his shoulder. His cock immediately leapt to life at the proximity of his mate. Great. So much for getting over the musk's effects. He'd begun to think that the worst was over, but one glimpse at his wife as she hung ass up, facedown over Lachlan's shoulder had his libido screaming back to life.

"Where's Matt?"

"Here," Matt said as he entered the room. He took a step toward Mikayla but then changed his mind and took a step away. Ryan entered the room behind him, and Matt held his arm out to hold him back. Ryan looked pissed at his brother's heavy handedness, but when he saw Mikayla, he too took a step away.

"Matt, it would seem that men aren't the only ones affected by the mating musk. Can I suggest you take a sample of blood before she recovers from the orgasms Brock and Bryce just gave her?"

Ty's cock throbbed painfully as images of Mikayla in the throes of climax rolled through his head. Matt must've been imagining them too because he seemed to shake himself before he nodded and moved quickly to grab the equipment. Lachlan lowered Mikayla to a sitting position, and that's when Ty noticed the ball gag. "Tried to bite me," Lachlan explained. Mikayla hummed as she tried to reach for Lachlan's cock. He moved out of the way and gave her a warning growl. She simply tried again.

"She's been edgy and impatient for the last few days, but it wasn't until she learned that three female medical researchers are on their way to the planet that she went completely berserk." Lachlan held her arms by her side even as he explained her behavior. "If Brock and Bryce hadn't been there to help me, I've would've had to tie her to the spanking bench." Mikayla made a noise so full of longing that Ty figured she really liked that idea.

A theory was working its way through Ty's brain, but he wasn't sure if it was based in fact or his own needs, but he voiced it anyway, looking to his twin for either confirmation or a smack upside the head.

"In the wild, mating musk is usually followed by frenzied mating." Lachlan raised an eyebrow daring him to finish that sentence. "I mean," Ty said carefully, "once the mating is done the musk's effects seem to dissipate quite rapidly."

"So you think that by all of you mating our wife, you'll all recover faster from the musk's effects?" Lachlan sounded skeptical, but he was smiling slightly.

"It's a fairly sound theory," Ryan added. "And I know that I feel in control enough that I'm no longer a danger to her. What about you, Ty?" Ty nodded, trying to discourage the erection tenting his pants. If they wanted to convince Lachlan that they were in control enough to keep Mikayla safe, it was probably best done without a cock hard enough to drive nails.

John and Peter walked into the lab, saw Mikayla, and both immediately turned around to leave.

"John, Peter," Lachlan called them back. "We have another issue."

Concern covering both their faces, they walked into the room, careful to stay as far away from Mikayla as possible.

"Mikayla wants to mate with all of you." The woman in question nodded her head enthusiastically. "Ryan and Ty think it's probably a way to lessen the musk's effect. We're expecting visitors, so I'm pretty sure our wife would be much happier if you were all back to normal."

Peter looked skeptical, but John looked willing to try just about anything to get over the mind-numbing effects of the musk's chemicals. Lachlan must've seen Peter's concern because he spoke as he removed the gag from Mikayla's mouth and touched her face lovingly.

"I'll stay as well, just in case anyone gets out of hand. Although," he said as he finally released Mikayla from his gentle hold, "I'm beginning to think it's not Mikayla who needs my protection."

She smiled at Lachlan, the type of smile that suggested evil intent, and then slid off the table and stalked toward Ty as she discarded her clothes. Naked, she moved into his arms, and he held her close, kissing her gently. She practically purred as Ryan moved up behind her and started kissing her neck and shoulders.

Determined to take it slowly, Ty kissed Mikayla's jaw, then her neck and then left a wet trail with his tongue as he lowered to worship her puckered nipples. She held his head to her breast as he sucked, licked, and nibbled on her hardened nubs. She grabbed at his shirt, dragging it over his head, but he latched back on to her breast the moment the material was clear. She pushed her hands behind her back and by Ryan's low groan Ty figured she was undoing the zipper on his pants.

Ty's cock throbbed in answer to his woman's need and he lowered his hands to release it from the confining denim. Mikayla lifted his head away from her breasts, her fingers insistent and demanding in his hair and pushed him lower to her mound. Pleased by her demand and more than eager to oblige, Ty thrust his tongue into her wet folds, separating the flesh and seeking the bundle of nerves that would send her excitement into overdrive.

She gasped as he found it, her taste delicious on his tongue as he tormented her over and over. She writhed at the sound of the lube bottle and then Ryan was thrusting his fingers in her ass, preparing her for his possession. Groaning, Mikayla dragged Ty by his hair once more, her leg wrapping around his hip as she offered him her pussy. He quickly shoved the material of his jeans out of the way and plunged into her hot, wet slit.

Ryan lifted her off her feet as he thrust into her ass. Suspended between them she sighed contentedly and held still for a moment before kissing him softly and issuing a single demand. "Fuck me."

Ryan chuckled, but they both did as the lady requested. Thrusting harder, deeper into her body Ty panted as his excitement curled higher. He could feel the walls of her pussy grabbing at his cock, trying to hold him inside her. He could feel Ryan as he thrust in counterpoint, and then he could feel nothing but frantic need as his desire to claim his woman, to mark her as his own, overwhelmed him.

Grunting with the effort, Ty was barely aware of his brother's identical noises, but when Mikayla exploded into a writhing orgasm, he couldn't hear anything but the roaring in his own ears. He pushed into her one more time, and then his cum pulsed from him, the orgasm going on and on. He felt Ryan follow a moment later. With the three of them pressed together panting hard, Ty had forgotten about their audience until John cleared his throat behind him.

* * * *

John could barely think past the need to fill Mikayla's mouth with his cock. Watching Ryan and Ty take her together had ramped his desire far higher than any stupid musk could do. He held Mikayla as Ryan and Ty carefully extricated their cocks and then lifted her into his arms.

She moaned in delight and nipped at his jaw. "Watch those teeth, princess. I'm about to fill that mouth with something I'd rather you not bite." She giggled happily, and he leaned forward to kiss her reverently. Whether she was affected by the musk or not she was definitely the perfect match for them all—loving, creative, adventurous, sexy as hell.

He glanced over at Peter realizing that his brother already had the lube out and was slicking it over his hard cock. John raised an eyebrow at Matt who grinned back, lifted his naked ass onto the low bench, and held his arms out for Mikayla. She crawled onto him quickly lowering onto his cock. John moved to the other side of the bench, nudged his brother so that he lay sort of diagonally across the bench and then tapped his cock against his wife's delectable lips. She flicked out her tongue, teasing the slit and nibbling the head but she squeaked in surprise when Peter pushed into her ass.

"Peter?" she asked quietly.

Peter looked worried, but a moment later his face broke into a brilliant smile when his bossy wife ordered her husbands around once more. "Thank god, now fuck me, please."

The three of them tried to build a rhythm but the angle was awkward, the table probably uncomfortable, and John had to keep shoving Matt out of the way so that he didn't accidentally end up rubbing his balls on his brother's face. In the end the four of them were so busy laughing that Mikayla's orgasm took them all by surprise.

She hummed against John's cock, sucking him deep, holding him captive until he groaned and gave her his cum. He heard his brothers' grunts as they plunged in and out of her body, and then they, too, followed their wife into bliss.

Stunned by the awkward but rather satisfying foursome, John moaned as Lachlan moved to extract Mikayla from the sweaty clinch.

"Happy now?" Lachlan asked Mikayla. She nodded sleepily, and John watched as Lachlan lifted her against his chest and told her to say goodnight to her husbands. Considering it was only just past midday, John figured that they wouldn't be seeing their wife at dinner today.

He watched Lachlan cradle her close and realized that whatever problem had been dealing with since Mikayla's miscarriage he seemed to have gotten over it. John shook his head. About time.

Chapter Nine

Mikayla snuggled into Lachlan's embrace. She was sweaty and sticky, and stuff was starting to dry in uncomfortable places. She'd never been so happy to hear the shower running in her entire life. Lachlan helped her to her feet and held her hand to balance her as she stepped into the shower stall. She turned her face into the warm water, letting it soothe her from head to foot.

After a moment she felt Lachlan step in behind her. Relieved, pleased, and already needy for the man who'd denied them both for so long, she turned and wrapped her arms around his waist.

"Thank you," she whispered.

"Little one," he chuckled as he worked shampoo into her hair, "I just watched you make love to all seven of my brothers. Did you really think I'd be able to resist you after that?"

She shrugged her shoulders, not willing to admit that she'd actually thought he could. He'd been so strong, so stubborn over the last few months that she really didn't know what to believe. "Although," he said on a quiet chuckle, "I think maybe I'll avoid foursomes. God, I thought Peter was going to fall off the table he was laughing so hard."

She giggled at that. It had felt rather strange, considering the man had his cock up her ass at the time, but the orgasm the movement set off had been quite enlightening.

They fell silent for a moment. "Lachlan, you do know the miscarriage wasn't your fault, right?" She said the words slowly, not wanting to break the mood but finally feeling the time had come. She needed to know why he'd pulled away from her over the last few months. Lachlan had been reticent to make love to her when she was pregnant, but they hadn't been intimate at all since her miscarriage.

"I'm sorry I wasn't there for you," he said, not actually agreeing with her statement. He looked so sad that for a moment she couldn't form words. She'd been fairly certain that his protective nature had made him feel like he'd let her down, but having it confirmed made her ache for him.

"You were," she said. He raised an eyebrow in disbelief. "What I mean is, you were on the ice planet rescuing Brock. You were exactly where I needed you to be at the time." He nodded slowly as if he hadn't thought of that angle. She knew without a shadow of a doubt that he would've been with her if circumstance had allowed.

"But I'm still sorry I wasn't there for you."

"Okay, how about next time I get pregnant," she said as she tried to swallow her fear of another miscarriage, "you and the rest of my husbands make sure to stay on the same planet with me."

"Deal," he said in a rough voice as he touched her face with his fingertips. "I love you, Mikayla."

"I love you, too, Lachlan."

She pressed a soft kiss to his lips, and then he eased her into the stream of water, rinsed the shampoo from her hair, and then ran the soap over her back and shoulders. He lowered to his knees taking his time to clean her in ways only a Dom would consider his duty, and then he stood and quickly washed himself down.

A few minutes later, sitting cross-legged on the bed, Lachlan sat behind her to dry her hair more thoroughly. "I should whip your ass for lying," he said as he tugged on her hair hard enough to get her full attention.

"Lying?" she asked in a squeaky voice. It figured that the one time she wasn't angling for a spanking she would manage to earn one.

"Yes, lying. Did you think you would fool me, little one?"

She shrugged not really wanting to dig herself into a hole.

"Aren't you going to try and convince me I'm wrong?" he asked as he pushed her forward so that her shoulders and face rested on the mattress and her ass lifted into the air. He ran a warm hand over her bottom, stroking over the flesh he was threatening to whip.

"Well, I was affected by the musk in a way." He grunted and leaned over her to laugh quietly in her ear.

"And how did you figure that, little one." He pressed his hard cock against her ass, and she had trouble remembering the darn question.

"My husbands needed help and, well...um." She moaned as he rubbed his cock up and down her slit. "Um...I couldn't leave them like that with three other females about to land on the planet."

"I see," he said, sliding his cock slowly into her pussy. "The musk made you territorial, and you had to fight for your men." He pulled out and slid back in slowly.

"That's right," she managed to gasp. "I was protecting my men just like you all protect me." He surged into her pussy, slapping his balls against her skin and then holding still.

"So the sex with Bryce and Brock who weren't affected by the musk was what?"

She felt her muscles flutter around his invasion as she tried to concentrate enough not to admit to her deception. She groaned as he pulled out of her completely and then pressed back in hard.

"Tell me," he taunted. "Explain to me how you were protecting Bryce and Brock by fucking them both so hard they could barely move afterward." He chuckled in her ear. "Tell me how you knew that fucking the others in the lab the way you did would take the edge off their lust." She groaned as he began pounding into her harder, deeper. She gasped as he ground his cock inside her, pressing her clit hard against the mattress and raising her desire a whole lot higher.

"Tell me again," he panted close to her ear, suddenly very serious. "Tell me again how much you love me."

Her orgasm started before she could get the words out, and Lachlan plunged into her over and over as his excitement grew. She screamed as every muscle in her body shook with her release. She panted as she felt his cum pulse deep into her body, and she felt tears spill from her eyes when he whispered how much he loved her.

He pulled his cock from her body and rolled her over carefully. Warm fingers wiped away the tears on her face, and his soft voice pleaded one more time. "Tell me."

"I will love you until the end of time. You're mine, Lachlan Davidson, and don't you ever forget it."

He smiled, leaned over to kiss her softly, and then pulled her back into his arms. They lay quietly together for a moment, but then he chuckled and said, "Don't think this gets you out of a whipping. You lied to me, little one, so you'll pay tomorrow."

She snuggled closer. She could barely wait.

Epilogue

It felt strange to have neighbors. Even on the ice planet that had essentially been an established mining colony, she hadn't had any actual neighbors. Now they had a second, smaller research station basically parked at their front door. Thankfully the three female medical scientists had quickly identified the chemical part of the creature's mating musk that affected humans and discovered its effects could be overcome by daily doses of a simple, specially blended multivitamin elixir.

The women had used so many medical terms when explaining the problem and cure that Mikayla had barely understood a word. Still feeling a little territorial over her men, she'd contacted Tracey, who'd contacted a medical friend, who'd explained that the science behind the discovery seemed solid. So now, Mikayla breathed a little easier.

It wasn't that she didn't trust her men to be faithful, but after seeing them affected by the mating musk, she didn't want there to be any misunderstandings between them and three unattached women. The fact that the women had more in common with her highly educated husbands hadn't missed Mikayla's notice either.

"What is that delicious smell?" Bryce came into the kitchen with a broad smile on his face. She enjoyed cooking, but she wasn't exactly a master chef.

"Just pot roast," she said as he pulled her into his embrace. He still limped on his damaged leg but stubbornly refused to get it fixed. There was a procedure that would easily replace the damaged thigh and hip bone with a polymer implant, but it meant several days in hospital and weeks of physical therapy. Bryce had simply refused to go back to Earth to get it done. Considering what happened last time they were in a hospital, she couldn't blame him for his reticence.

"Nope," he said against her hair, "the delicious smell is far sweeter than pot roast. It must be you." She giggled as he kissed and nibbled her ear for a moment, but then Matt seemed to grow serious.

"I'm sorry we didn't figure it out sooner," he said as Bryce hugged her closer. "Are you okay?"

She looked at Matt, wondering how the hell he could think she wasn't okay. "Matt, I'm fine. More than fine. None of you did anything to scare me. Hell, I was more concerned that my husbands were pulling away, and I didn't know why."

"I can't describe how intense and immediate the pheromone's effects were. It was kind of frightening. I'm really glad I wasn't anywhere near you at the time."

He looked so remorseful that she couldn't decide whether to drag him into a hug or verbally smack him upside the head. The guy not only got a full dose of the mating musk at its strongest, but he managed to stay calm enough to identify and remove the source. It didn't matter how wild his need for her had been, he'd recognized the symptoms immediately and controlled himself.

But gentle reassurance never worked with this husband. She eased out of Bryce's embrace, marched over to Matt, and waved a finger in his face. "Matt Davidson, you are, *seriously*, the biggest pain in the ass." The look on his face would've been comical if his remorse hadn't been so ridiculous. Bryce laughed behind her as she said, "Matt, you did everything right, so stop with the guilt already."

"Finally," Bryce said with a laugh, "the voice of reason."

Matt grabbed her hand, held it to his heart for a moment as understanding flowed between them.

"I love you, Mikayla," he said as he touched her face with the back of his knuckles.

"I love you, too. Now take me to bed," she said in the bossiest tone she could muster. Bryce smiled at her words, and after a moment of surprise, Matt grinned also. He winked, lifted her in his arms, and whispered two words, "Yes, ma'am."

End of Book 3: Wild Fascination

To be continued in
Book 4: Keen Inclination

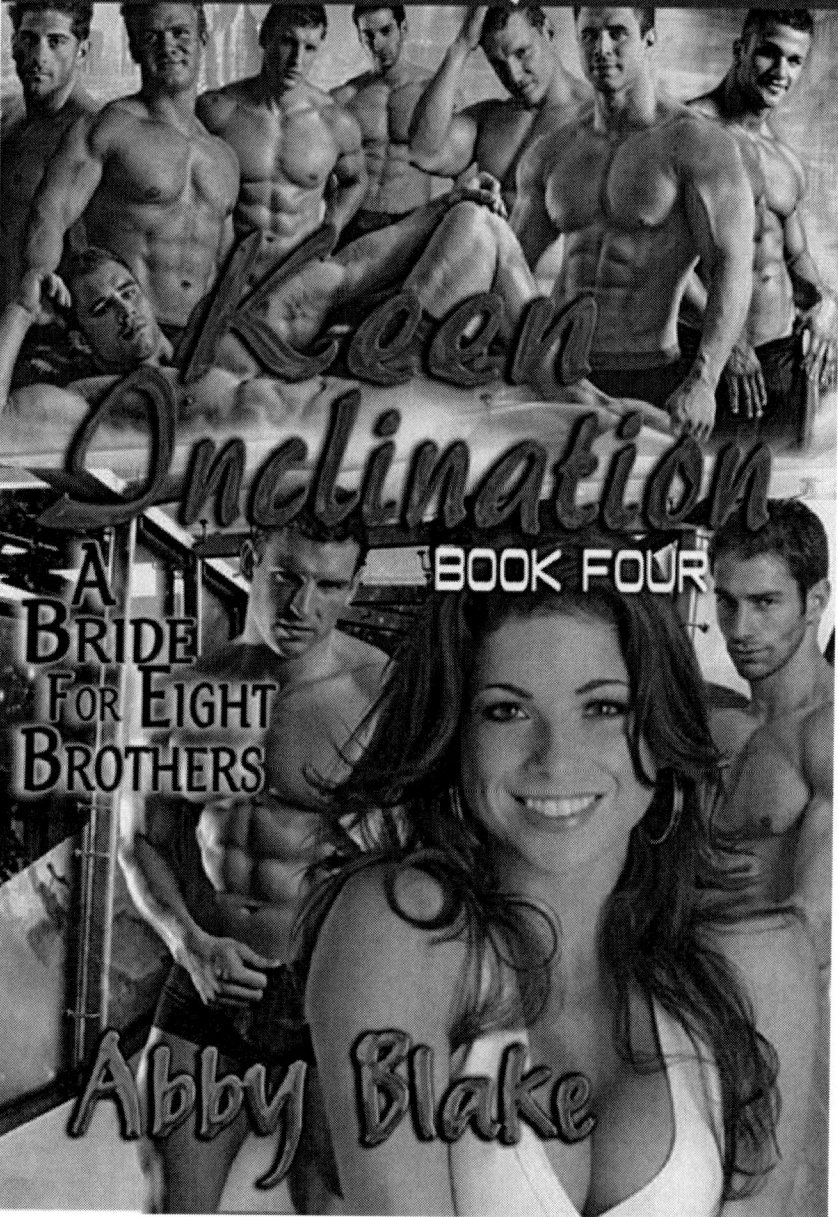

KEEN INCLINATION

A Bride for Eight Brothers 4

ABBY BLAKE
Copyright © 2011

Chapter One

Mikayla hummed to herself as she peeled the vegetables for dinner. Tonight the researchers from the base next door were coming for the evening meal, and she hoped the happy sound masked her apprehension. Her men knew exactly how she felt about having other women around them on a planet occupied with tiny critters that could affect a man's libido, but it would've been very rude to turn the medical research scientists away. And besides, as Bryce not so tactfully pointed out, her men were working with these women on a daily basis, so not having them at her dinner table only affected her chances at making friends, not their contact with her men.

It would've been nice to have some female company, but she had very little in common with the medical scientists. The few times Mikayla had spent any time with them she'd been awkward and shy and maybe a little intimidated. Jacqueline seemed especially dismissive and always left Mikayla feeling unwelcome, even in her own home. And okay, as long as Mikayla was being honest with herself, maybe she hadn't been quite as welcoming as she could've been. But it didn't help that the three women had worked together for years or that they knew each other so well or that Mikayla felt like she had nothing in common with any of them. Peter's ex-fiancée and the hell she'd put them through was probably a factor as well.

Feeling a little anxious over what should be a family dinner plus three seemed silly even to her own mind, but she couldn't shake the disquiet.

"Do you need any help?" Ryan asked as he and Ty came into the room.

"Thanks, but I've got everything under control." They were sweet to ask, but at least with the excuse of having to prepare dinner she could put off having to worry how she would deal with their guests. "They're due at six, right?" she asked, hoping against hope that the women had somehow needed to cancel.

"Just arrived," Ryan said cheerfully, but Mikayla could hear the strain in his voice. Their guests weren't supposed to be here for at least another hour, and by turning up early they gave the subtle inference that Mikayla wasn't quite up to standard. She tried to rein in the bitchy thoughts. God, just because she felt intimidated by the women, it didn't mean they'd gone out of their way to make her feel inadequate.

Ty wrapped his arms around her, almost as if he could see into her mind and all the insecurities swirling inside. "It's going to be fine," he said reassuringly. "The others can keep them entertained while we help with dinner."

Oh, so, fucking fabulous. Not only was she going to worry about dinner being perceived as served late, she also got the chance to fret over why three women would turn up early to spend social time with her husbands.

She slammed the vegetables onto the chopping board, her irritation growing with every slice. Why her husbands had actually invited the women was completely beyond her anyway. Matt and Bryce, and Ryan and Ty spent more than enough time working with the women during the day. Wasn't that enough?

"Maybe," Ty said in a suspiciously casual voice, "we should cook dinner, and you can go spend some time with our guests."

"No," she said just a tad too quickly. It seemed so ridiculous that she felt this way, but she couldn't shake the feeling of inadequacy. She was damned if she would hand over her favorite chore to Ryan and Ty just so she could go supervise three bitchy women who were probably making a play for her husbands as she stood in the kitchen argu— "I mean, yes. That would be wonderful. You two can cook and I'll go supervi...I mean socialize with our guests." Ryan's lips quirked at her slip, but he nodded and grabbed the knife she'd been using.

"Not a problem," Ty said as he washed his hands. She watched a moment longer as her men quickly took over then turned to the dining room, determined to be a perfect hostess.

As she entered the room, it quickly became apparent that Jacqueline was holding court as if she were some kind of royalty. Six of Mikayla's husbands sat around the table listening to the woman as if she were the most fascinating thing on the planet.

"So I ran a complete chemical analysis and found that the combination of pheromones rather than a single chemical is what increases the potency of the mating musk." Jacqueline flicked her blonde curls over her shoulder and leaned closer to Peter.

"Hi," Mikayla said, feeling uncomfortable in her own dining room. "Can I get anybody a drink?" Jacqueline glanced in her general direction without actually looking at her, dismissed Mikayla with a flick of her fingers, and continued talking. Mikayla tried very hard not to take offense, but no matter what argument she came up with, she couldn't convince herself that Jacqueline's behavior was because of her quirky scientific brain and not some deliberate attempt to be offensive. The woman leaned closer to Peter and touched his arm

"So I double-checked the base compounds and found that the musk can't be created artificially. There isn't anything on Earth that could be used to synthesize an equivalent, so the only way to make what the medical consortium wants is to cultivate the Apodemus Non-terra Melanurus. Unfortunately, we haven't been able to adequately replicate the natural environment for it to produce the pheromones we need."

Mikayla wanted to roll her eyes at the woman's self-absorbed behavior. Why didn't she just use the word "mouse" like everyone else? She seemed to be deliberately using scientific words in an attempt to make Mikayla look stupid. Perhaps Jacqueline missed the part that Mikayla had been working side by side with Ryan and Ty when they named the furry critter. But unfortunately, none of her husbands seemed to notice the snub, and the fact that her men seemed to be hanging on Jacqueline's every word just served to piss Mikayla off more. She noticed the other two women hanging back, staying out of Jacqueline's way, and headed over to ask them if they would like a drink.

Without showing any indication that she'd seen Mikayla move, Jacqueline called the other two women into the conversation, effectively leaving Mikayla standing alone once more. It didn't escape her notice that Misha and Keira practically ran away from her in the process.

Lachlan watched her for a moment but went back to listening when Jacqueline asked him a question about the geological terrain or something equally as boring. Mikayla was trying to slip away when Bryce caught her arm and hauled her onto his lap. As comfortable as she usually felt sitting on her husbands' laps, tonight it felt like the equivalent of being relegated to the kiddy table. She wasn't part of the conversation, she wasn't expected to participate, and it felt worse than hiding in the kitchen and worrying about her men.

She cuddled into Bryce for a few moments and tried to find her self-confidence. She was a happily married woman, and she trusted her husbands to remain faithful. There were no mouse tears on the base, and even if there were, she knew her husbands well enough to know they'd do everything in their power to resist the mating musk's influence. Hell, they'd practically turned themselves inside out trying to protect her when they'd first arrived on the planet. She had no reason to believe they wouldn't do the same if it happened again.

Feeling better than she had in quite a while, Mikayla leaned up to kiss Bryce on the cheek, whispered a thank you in his ear, and headed back to the kitchen.

She just needed to get through this dinner.

* * * *

Finally, the longest meal in history was done. Mikayla actually looked forward to doing the dishes and putting the whole damn thing behind her. Peter hadn't yet come back to the kitchen after escorting the female scientists to the door, and even though Mikayla was a little annoyed at being left with the chore, she was also grateful for the time alone.

It was probably pretty silly, but being married to eight men meant alone time was rare and precious. And for some reason, something she craved more and more lately.

"There's my princess," John said as he entered the kitchen with Brock and Lachlan. She smiled to hide her reaction to being no longer alone as John stalked closer. He grinned, acting for all the world like he was a hunter and she was his prey. "Change of plans." He wrapped his arms around her and lifted her off her feet. "Brock and Lachlan are going to break some dishes—"

Brock interrupted with an affronted-sounding, "Hey."

John rolled his eyes but amended his words. "Brock and Lachaln are going to finish doing the dishes because you, my lovely princess, are needed elsewhere."

John lifted her higher and wrapped her legs around his waist. "So, change of plans."

"Why?" she asked, trying to ignore the very hard cock pressing against her crotch.

"Do I need a reason to want to spend some quality time with my wife?" He said it with a smile on his face, but she couldn't help noticing that he wanted an answer.

"No," she said as she pressed a kiss to his cheek. "I'm just a little wiped out is all. It's been a long day."

He grinned, pulled her closer, and started walking from the kitchen. "That, princess, is exactly why there is a change of plans."

He kissed her all the way back to his living quarters, slow, delicious, drugging kisses that made her feel pliant and relaxed in his arms. When they entered his rooms, she was surprised to find the area lit with tiny little lights that flickered in a similar way to candles. She knew they weren't actual candles—the station's safety devices would have detected open flame and moved to extinguish the danger—but they created the same ambiance.

John carried her straight to the bathroom, where they found Peter preparing a hot bubble bath. The delicious smell of vanilla filled the small area, and she couldn't help but wonder how long they'd been planning this.

"Perfect timing," Peter said as he stepped closer, lifted her from John's arms and pressed a kiss to her mouth. He smiled as he stripped her clothes off, and then, with his usual fastidiousness, folded them neatly.

John held a hand out and steadied her as she stepped into the gloriously hot water. It took a few moments to adjust to the temperature, but then Mikayla leaned back and closed her eyes, simply enjoying the water's caress.

The bath wasn't very big, so it didn't surprise her that neither of the men tried to join her in the water. Already feeling calmer, Mikayla half opened her eyes as Peter pressed a soft washcloth to her skin. He worked the vanilla-scented bath wash over her arms and shoulders, stopping to massage the tight muscles of her neck, before easing her forward and continuing the sensuous movement down her back.

She couldn't help but moan in relief as muscles she'd held tight through the entire dinner finally began to loosen. Peter stopped what he was doing, wrapped his arms around her upper body and kissed the back of her neck.

"We know tonight was difficult for you, but they're quite nice people once you get to know them." Mikayla wasn't so sure, but she kept that thought to herself.

Peter held her a moment longer then resumed his movements with the washcloth. When he was finished, John stepped closer with a large towel, helped her out of the bath, and very slowly rubbed her dry. By the time he was finished, she was feeling very, very awake. He grinned when he saw her face then bent and swung her into his arms.

Naked, the three of them stretched out on John's bed. Mikayla tried not to react to Peter's decision to stay. Until recently, he'd been a very private lover, taking her gently, reverently, and never sharing their time together with one of his brothers, but since the mouse tears pheromone had affected him, he'd been more willing to show her his kinky side. Mikayla was very glad to know the true man inside, but even under the mouse tears influence, he'd still been the one to show her the gentler side to kinky sex.

They encouraged her to snuggle into John's embrace, and then Peter smoothed a scented cream over her arms and shoulders, down her spine, over her ass, and down to the end of her feet. She writhed with the soothing sensation, feeling both relaxed and energized at the same time. John helped her to roll over, and Peter repeated the process, taking special care with her breasts and her belly and then lower between her thighs.

Moaning now with need, Mikayla gasped when Peter lowered his mouth over her pussy, pushed her thighs wide, and laved her like ice cream. Over and over he licked the wet folds, teasing the sensitive flesh until she growled her need. Two masculine chuckles reached her ears a moment before Peter thrust his hard tongue deep into her core, fucking her as John held her close.

Her legs quivered, her pussy pulsed, her breathing jammed in her throat. Peter held her there, licking slowly once more, humming against her swollen clit as she writhed with need. John smoothed his hands over her aching nipples, toying with the sensitive nubs until she thought she'd explode. But then they stopped, pulled away, and grinned as she growled at them both.

As soon as her arousal dropped from boiling to simmer, they started again, John caressing her stomach and breasts, Peter tongue-fucking her until she could barely remember her own name.

But when they stopped again, she writhed frantically in their hold. Hell, this was the sort of thing Brock and Lachlan usually did. Had the brothers been sharing notes?

"Please," she begged, unable to force more than that one simple word past her lips.

"Shhh, princess, we'll take care of you," John said as he brushed a hand through her hair.

"Now?" she asked, uncaring that the word was breathless with desperation.

"Yes, now," Peter answered as he surged over her and slid his cock deep inside her hungry pussy.

But he loved her slowly, his thrusts relaxed and lazy. He grinned when she tried to lift her hips, trying to claim more of him, trying to speed their race to orgasm. When he pulled away, she damn near whimpered at the loss, but John lifted and rolled her over his body, and she quickly slid down to impale herself on his waiting cock. She sighed as he thrust up to meet her, fucking her harder, faster, deeper.

She was at the brink, ready to fall over the edge, when John stopped all movement and held her down. Mikayla could barely breathe. With her swollen clit trapped between them, her arousal continued to climb. Even without moving, her orgasm swelled closer. Her men must've sensed just how near she was because she heard the hurried squirt of lube and then felt Peter push quickly into her back passage. All three of them held still as her climax rushed closer.

And then, like an elastic breaking under tension, her orgasm snapped, shaking every muscle, rasping every nerve, sending heat through every vein in her body. She gasped as they held her tight between them, both men groaning as her ass and pussy caressed their hard cocks.

Finally, she lay quietly in their hold, warmth melting through her as exhaustion tried to claim her. But then her men started to move, Peter sliding into her ass as John lifted her off his cock. Up and down, again and again, over and over, they slid their hard cocks into her body. She quickly went from exhausted to excited, completely spent but totally needy.

She felt another orgasm building deep, and she damn near screamed when Peter leaned over and bit her ear. "Are you ready?" he asked wickedly.

Ready for what? But her unasked question was answered as both her men started to pound into her body. No longer controlled, no longer restrained, they fucked her harder, faster, their rhythm broken, their breathing harsh.

Peter thrust hard into her ass, ramming his cock deep into her back passage as his climax claimed him. His movement drove her clit hard against John, her orgasm so unexpected that she screamed her surprise. John gripped her hips, grinding her against his pelvis, wringing every shiver from her release as his cock pulsed and throbbed inside her.

Finally, absolutely and completely exhausted, Mikayla closed her eyes, wanting nothing more than to sleep. Slowly, carefully, Peter pulled his softening cock from her ass, and John pressed a kiss to her forehead. She barely felt the washcloth as Peter cleaned her up, and she mourned the loss as John moved away for a brief moment.

She fell asleep in their arms, very glad that Peter chose to stay.

* * * *

John held his wife as she slept. He'd been very worried for her tonight. They'd invited the medical scientists so that Mikayla would have some female company, but maybe it hadn't been the smartest decision they'd made recently.

Jacqueline was a rather typical example of some of the personalities they encountered in their field of science. She was highly educated, extremely intelligent, and unless she was talking about her research, completely antisocial.

It was probably unfair for the brothers to expect Mikayla to understand the woman's quirks. Mikayla was sociable and accepting—practically the opposite of Jacqueline and the other researchers from the medical consortium—and though Mikayla had tried tonight, she hadn't quite been able to find common ground. Unfortunately, it would also seem that Jacqueline hadn't tried at all to get along with their wife. If anything, she'd become territorial when Mikayla had tried to engage Misha and Keira in conversation.

Maybe the brothers should've listened to Bryce. Having been an undercover cop for almost ten years, his instincts about other people were very well developed. He'd labeled Jacqueline a first-class bitch almost from the moment he'd met her, and no amount of explanation from his brothers had changed his mind. Considering that Jacqueline had seemed to go out of her way to make Mikayla feel unwelcome in her own home tonight, John was beginning to agree with Bryce.

Over the last few months, Mikayla hadn't really seemed herself, and all of the brothers had commented on the loss of her usual happy demeanor. Ironically, it had been the reason for tonight's dinner. They had hoped that by getting to know the medical scientists better, Mikayla might forge a friendship or at least an understanding with the other women, but in actuality it had probably been a humungous mistake.

"Peter? Are you asleep?" John asked in a soft whisper. Peter lifted his head from the pillow and looked at him in the dim light. The flickering pretend-candlelight might've been good for setting the mood, but it certainly didn't help a person see clearly. "I'm going to go talk to the others and make sure we don't have a repeat of tonight."

Peter nodded his agreement and pulled Mikayla closer.

It didn't take John long to find his brothers. They were all gathered in the dining room discussing the exact subject he'd planned to raise.

"Could it still be from the miscarriage?" Brock asked Matt as John walked in the door.

Matt shook his head slowly. With his background in pathology, he at least had some understanding of how pregnancy and hormones affected the female body. "Her hormones should've returned to normal months ago. It's more likely that she's still grieving in an emotional sense."

"So what do we do?" Ryan asked. "How can we help her?"

"Well, for starters we can make certain never to invite Jacqueline and her minions for dinner again." Lachlan and Bryce both smirked at John's description, but none of the brothers actually disagreed with his suggestion.

"How about we just make certain that she knows her husbands love her," Bryce said quietly. "I reckon her miscarriage probably undermined her confidence as a woman. The last thing she needs is the type of hostility Jacqueline projected tonight."

Whether Jacqueline's behavior was intentionally offensive or not didn't really matter. What mattered was how it affected Mikayla.

"Okay," John said, feeling a little better that his brothers agreed with his assessment of the situation. "We keep Mikayla close, show her how much we all love her, and just be there for her if she needs us."

They nodded in agreement. Unwilling to stay a moment longer when he could be holding his wife in his arms, John left and headed back to his room.

Chapter Two

Nearly six months later...

The loud, clanging alarm was the most fucking annoying, unwelcome sound in the history of the planet. This was at least the third time this week. Quickly, Lachlan reached for his gun and went to investigate.

Ever since word of the mouse tears mating musk had hit the intergalactic news stations, every moron and his friend had landed on the planet trying to capture a little mouse of their own. The most irritating thing was that none of them understood the overwhelming effect the musk had on human males.

When Lachlan had gone to investigate the last alert, he'd found two men frantically jacking off. It was not something he wanted to see again, but he suspected it was about to become part of his daily routine. The men had been practically cross-eyed with arousal, and it was only a matter of time before they'd turned to each other. Lachlan was fairly certain that hadn't been their intention when they'd gone looking for the furry little creature.

He'd grabbed both men and dragged them back to their sorry excuse for a space cruiser. With little fuss, he'd managed to set the controls to auto-lift and then watched as they left the atmosphere. They were probably still revolving around the planet in synchronous orbit, but hopefully, they were smart enough to leave once the musk's effects wore off.

"Have we got a location?" he asked Bryce as they met in the hallway.

"Less than three hundred yards from the aft border." This stupid planet had so much interference that they couldn't clearly detect the magnetic pole, so they had to use the same descriptions they used when the main station was in transport and technically considered a ship. Side by side they ran to the back exit of the building. Lachlan was pleased to see Bryce carried both a stun weapon and a traditional military issue handgun this time.

Even though they both preferred bullets over stun bolts, they didn't really want to hurt anybody. Half the time the invaders behind the incursions needed rescuing rather than shooting, but it didn't mean Lachlan or Bryce would hesitate to use deadly force if Mikayla or the female scientists were in danger.

* * * *

"Where's Mikayla?" Brock asked as the alarm sounded.

Ryan and Ty were already moving toward the weapons cabinets. Fortunately, none of the raiders had entered the compound so they hadn't needed to use the stun guns yet. But they were fully prepared to defend their home if the need arose.

Ty glanced at the time. "She should be in the kitchen," he said as he strapped the weapon holster to his shoulders. Brock nodded and headed out the door, checking that his stun gun was still fully charged. He, Lachlan, and Bryce had decided to carry a weapon at all times. Peter and John had no experience but were quickly learning how to use a stun gun. Ryan and Ty both had shooting experience, mainly with tranquilizer darts, but the very nature of their work in the lab made carrying a weapon dangerous. An accidental discharge of an electronic weapon inside the lab could result in severe damage to the lab and any occupants, humans included.

Brock called his wife as he entered the kitchen. She didn't answer. A quick glance around the room found half-peeled vegetables but no Mikayla. It seemed strange that she would leave dinner partially prepared, and concerns he hadn't considered for a few weeks made a way back into his thoughts. He headed to John's office but met the man halfway. John went back to the offices to check there, and Brock turned toward the living quarters.

Each moment he couldn't find Mikayla ratcheted his concern tighter. Over the last few months, Brock and his brothers had watched their wife slowly lose her self-confidence, despite their best efforts to stop it. In some ways, it had happened so gradually that it was only when Brock remembered a particular moment from the past and compared that to the woman she was now that he noticed just how much she had changed. All of the brothers knew it would take time to recover emotionally from her miscarriage. They'd minimized her contact with the female scientists as best they could, but Brock couldn't help feel there was more to it now.

But right at this moment, she had to be on the base. She knew she was supposed to stay with one of her husbands or be in the kitchen. When the raiders had started arriving, they'd all been in agreement, Mikayla included, that they would create a protocol and stick to it.

He went to the intercom unit on the wall just inside his quarters. He buzzed each room in the building until his brothers checked in. Ryan and Ty were still near the lab, and Matt was inside the communications room monitoring the invaders' movements. Brock had seen Lachlan and Bryce head out the back door, so he knew if she wasn't with Peter or John that they had a serious problem.

Feeling a little panicked, Brock did a quick sweep of his and Lachlan's quarters and was about to move to Matt and Bryce's when he heard a soft noise in the bathroom. He called her name, but Mikayla didn't answer. Weapon raised, he headed cautiously through the doorway.

* * * *

The raiders weren't hard to find. The three men were already affected by the musk and were literally rubbing themselves raw. One was even trying to hump a tree. Lachlan didn't even want to think about the splinters that would cause.

He pulled out his electric gun and stunned splinter-boy almost out of mercy. The other two seemed barely aware of his and Bryce's presence and in the end needed to be stunned as well.

"I've been in some pretty dangerous life or death situations," Bryce said on a deep laugh, "but I didn't think I would ever be involved in something as fucked up as this."

Lachlan nodded his agreement. It was looking more and more unlikely that the proposed mining would go ahead. Unless they could find an exclusively female workforce, chances were that the mineral ores weren't plentiful enough to deal with the chaos that the mating musk would cause.

The fact that the company the female scientists worked for had sworn him and his brothers to confidentiality, and threatened to withdraw the vitamin supplement if they'd refused, just made the whole thing more frustrating. The supplement was the only weapon they had to combat the mating musk's effects. Add that to the fact that the company decided against arranging for security to protect their staff—effectively leaving the women vulnerable to attack—and Lachlan was ready to break their contract and get his family the hell off this strange jungle planet.

Unfortunately, he wouldn't leave the three female scientists alone to deal with the raiders, and it would seem by the smug attitude of the decision makers at the medical research company that they knew it, too. It didn't help that his time in the defense forces had left him with a publicly available download listing his exemplary service history and supposedly heroic deeds. He didn't feel like a hero. He felt like a man who'd lived through a nightmare and barely returned whole.

The worst of the current situation was that sooner or later somebody was going to end up dead, and Lachlan sure as hell hoped it wasn't him who had to pull the trigger. He'd had to kill enough people to last him a lifetime. He suspected Bryce felt the same way.

It took a little longer to locate the ship belonging to these guys— they'd hidden it under several layers of vegetation—but Lachlan's tracking skills were becoming quite adept on this planet, and they found it eventually.

By the time they made it back to the three unconscious men, they were masturbating in their sleep. "We really should volunteer someone else for this part of the job," Bryce said as he grabbed one of the men and swung him onto his shoulders in a fireman's hold while trying not to touch anything that wasn't inside the man's clothing. Helpfully, the unconscious man still had his hand wrapped firmly around his dick.

With two heavy unconscious raiders of his own to carry, Lachlan decided to drag them both back by their collars. At least if they ended up with a bruise or two on their collective asses they might think twice about coming back.

The ship's systems had been password-disabled, but it only took a few moments for Bryce to break into the software. Obviously, his time as an undercover cop had given him skills few would consider necessary for honest folk, but they were coming in very handy on this planet.

They stood back as the ship lifted off the ground and headed into orbit. Hopefully, the raiders would wake sore and sorry in a few hours and decide that the mouse tears just weren't worth the risk.

* * * *

Brock found Mikayla in the bath. The headset from her music player was turned up so loud he could hear the song from the doorway.

"Baby girl," he said as he knelt down and touched her hair softly. She practically leapt out of the bath at his soft caress.

"Shit, Brock," she said breathlessly as she pulled the headphones from her ears. "Talk about giving a girl a heart attack."

"Mikayla," he said quietly, "what are you doing?"

At first it looked like she would give him some smartass answer, but then she took a deep breath, shrugged slightly, and said, "I just needed a little bit of time to myself." She looked away from him, trying to hide the tears in her eyes, and he found himself wondering if she was understating her need to hide. It certainly seemed that she was hiding, and considering the half-peeled vegetables, she was having trouble concentrating as well. None of them had known where she was, and that concerned him a great deal. With raiders landing on the planet, it was very important for everyone to know where everyone was.

But he'd been especially worried about his wife lately. It wasn't anything specific, just a feeling that she was pulling away from all of them in an emotional sense. Almost like she was rethinking the whole eight husbands thing. They hadn't really discussed trying for another baby. He planned to raise the subject when their access to medical care was adequate, but he wondered just how she really felt about risking another miscarriage. Just because it was unlikely that she would suffer a second ectopic pregnancy, it didn't guarantee it wouldn't happen.

The trouble was Brock really couldn't be certain how much was observation and how much was coming from his own insecurities, so he hadn't said anything to her. Most women only had to deal with one or two husbands, not eight. What would happen if Mikayla chose to leave some or all of them?

As he tried to figure out how best to protect her—from the current raiders *and* her own concerns—John barreled through the door and came to a sudden halt behind him.

"Hello, princess," he said with a lascivious grin. Brock didn't need to guess what his brother was thinking.

"Call the others. Tell them we found her." John gave him an annoyed look, but Brock just shook his head. Their brothers were busy dealing with intruders, so climbing into the bath with their lovely wife was probably not a responsible choice at the moment.

"Baby girl," Brock said as he ran a soothing hand up and down her spine. "John is going to stay with you while we sort out this latest batch of raiders. And then we're going to talk about what's going on in your head." She nodded and tried a sad smile, but it was obvious that whatever she'd been thinking before he came in was not good.

A knot formed in his stomach. Something told him things were changing. Somehow the idyllic life he thought they had together wasn't quite as solid as he'd once believed.

He helped her from the bath, dried her off, and sat her on the bed. "Stay," he said when it looked like she might follow him. John helped her get dressed and then lay down beside her and pulled her into his arms.

"I'll tell the others you two want some alone time, but I can't promise to keep Lachlan away. He'll know something's up the moment he sees me." She nodded again, not even trying to reassure him that everything was all right. Brock made eye contact with John, and then left the room quietly.

In the hallway, he took a deep breath, preparing himself to lie to his brothers and pretend that everything was fine.

Chapter Three

"Seriously?" Ryan asked and then laughed harder.

Lachlan was still trying to *not* imagine how many splinters humping a tree would cause when Brock came into the room. The man smiled and laughed with the rest of them as Bryce gave them all a very comical description of the three raiders they'd just sent home, but Lachlan could sense something wasn't quite right. He also realized that Brock wasn't in the mood to talk about it.

"I'm just glad it was a tree. I swear we're liable to find them humping each other one of these days. What part of 'quarantine' don't these dickheads understand?"

"Is the vitamin supplement still suppressing the pheromones' effects?" Brock asked, sounding very serious.

Lachlan glanced around the rest of his brothers. None of the others seemed to have noticed Brock's strange mood, so Lachlan answered the question quickly and resolved to get answers to his own questions later.

"It's still effective, but maybe not as effective as it once was. Either that, or the mouse tears are getting more potent. I would suggest that we consider not taking the supplement unless we're planning to leave the building. I don't want the only thing that inhibits the effects of the mating musk losing its potency."

"True," Ty said, still laughing. "Hell, we could all end up humping trees." He acted out a rather crude version of what could happen, and the rest of his brothers laughed with him.

"I suppose it makes sense," Ryan said, looking thoughtful. "I'll let Misha know."

"No, I'd rather the medical consortium didn't know. We'll continue to accept the weekly allocations, but we'll just store the excess. The way they have been acting lately, I wouldn't put it past them to cut off our supply if they felt it were in their company's best interest."

"We probably need to hire more security ourselves," Bryce said, concern creasing his face. "So far these raiders have come in small numbers. If we get a larger raiding party, we could be in trouble."

"Or the trees could," Ty added, still laughing.

"Oh, shit, what if there were enough of them to make a daisy chain?" Ryan added.

Lachlan shook his head in an effort to dislodge that image. He hoped like hell he'd never have to try and break up a group of mating musk affected men humping in a circle. Today's experience had been unpleasant enough.

"Where's Mikayla?" Bryce asked curiously as he finally stopped laughing.

"Spending some quiet time with John," Brock said, projecting a calm Lachlan was certain the man wasn't feeling. He watched as his brother tried to force a relaxed smile onto his face. "I volunteered to cook dinner."

They all groaned as Brock knew his brothers would and Lachlan watched curiously as Brock headed into the kitchen, thereby forestalling any more questions about their wife. Obviously something was amiss, but even more concerning was Brock's unwillingness to share.

He followed Brock into the kitchen and caught his brother's disappointed sigh.

"I think we should renegotiate our contract," Brock said as if to override any questions from Lachlan. Lachlan noticed the tension in Brock's shoulders and really wanted to demand answers. But Brock was a far better Dom than Lachlan, and if Lachlan pushed too hard, Brock would simply shut down and keep his secret forever.

"Sure," Lachlan answered carefully. "It's probably a good idea. We are spending more time on security than surveys and research."

"True," Brock said as if he hadn't actually considered that angle.

"Okay, I'll contact our lawyer," Lachlan said, watching his brother closely. Brock looked over at him but waited for Lachlan to elaborate. "If nothing else, it might at least alert the mining company to the medical consortium's attitude toward protecting its staff."

Brock nodded, and Lachlan could practically see his brother looking at the suggestion from all angles.

"Okay," he finally agreed. "In fact, it might be a good idea for John to head back to earth for a while. Maybe he could take Mikayla along."

"Only if you go with them," Lachlan said. He sure as hell didn't miss the relief in his brother's expression. Whatever was going on, Brock and John seemed inclined to keep it from the rest of them.

"Okay," Brock said again. "I think that would be a good idea. John and Mikayla and I will head back to Earth for a few weeks, renegotiate the contracts, and hopefully get us extra help with security."

Lachlan nodded, watched his brother's body language closely for a while, and then turned to leave the room.

"They're in my bed," Brock said quietly. Lachlan raised an eyebrow. It wasn't uncommon for the brothers to do a certain amount of bed-hopping to be with their wife, but usually, intimate alone time with Mikayla was done is their own beds, not someone else's. He waited for Brock to elaborate, but it seemed that he'd said all he was going to say. Lachlan nodded his thanks for what he expected was a cryptic clue and headed to his and Brock's living quarters.

* * * *

John lay on the bed, his arms wrapped around Mikayla. He'd held her for less than a minute before he realized she was trying hard not to cry.

"I'm sorry," she said quietly. "I don't know what's wrong with me. I just can't seem to fight it. I'm not even sure why I feel so sad."

Remorse cut through him, and he pulled her closer. He hadn't even noticed how much she'd withdrawn from them until today. With all the chaos of the mouse tears, the female scientists, and the constant arrival of raiders, he hadn't given any thought to how his wife might feel in the center of it all.

He was still trying to figure out what to do when the door opened quietly. John wasn't even surprised to see Lachlan. If any of his brothers had picked up on Mikayla's unusual behavior, it would be Lachlan. Irrational anger tromped through John's mind, unfairly blaming his brother for not alerting him to concerns he himself hadn't seen.

"Little one," Lachlan said, managing to sound both sad and annoyed at the same time. He leaned over and smoothed the hair away from Mikayla's eyes. "John and Brock are going to take you to Earth. We want you to see a doctor first and then spend some time relaxing."

She nodded tiredly, her eyes still closed. John couldn't help but wonder if Lachlan had noticed her gradual withdrawal why he hadn't done anything until now. His ability to read body language was sometimes a little freaky. But then again, the change had been so gradual maybe even Lachlan hadn't realized just how far she'd moved away from the vibrant, sassy woman they'd all fallen in love with.

Then the part about taking her to Earth sank in.

"Brock and I think it would be a good idea to renegotiate our contract," Lachlan said to him. John nodded. He'd been thinking the same thing ever since the raids had started. This was not the situation they'd signed up for, and it would be a plausible excuse for getting Mikayla off the planet without upsetting the others. Although, he suspected that, like him, his brothers would be happier to have her somewhere safer until they could sort out the security issues.

"I'll go run a systems check on the cruiser. Brock's driving," Lachlan said as he headed out the door. John nodded again and then pulled Mikayla closer.

"Hear that, princess? Big brother still won't let me fly the family spaceship." She smiled slightly, and he felt reassured by the fact that she hadn't withdrawn completely. She was hurting and very tired, but at least she was still acknowledging his presence. "It's not like I crashed it on purpose," he said on a pretend grumble, trying to inject a hint of "normal" into their conversation. She nodded slowly and then wriggled closer.

When he and his brothers had discussed buying their own intergalactic transport, John had nearly gagged at the exorbitant expense, but with the current situation, he was very glad his brothers had insisted. The trip back to Earth would take just over thirteen hours. If they had to wait for commercial shipping lines, it could've taken weeks to get Mikayla back to Earth.

"I've packed some things for Mikayla," Brock said as he came in the door. "Give me a minute to pack some stuff, and I'll get Mikayla to the cruiser while you grab some clothes."

John nodded and then leaned forward to press a kiss to his wife's cheek. "I love you," he whispered, unable to think of any way to reassure her more than he already had. Reluctantly, he rolled off the bed and let Brock lift Mikayla to her feet. John nodded once and then headed for the door.

* * * *

Lachlan watched his normally controlled brother practically twitch with agitation as he filled him in on the last twenty-four hours since they'd left the jungle planet.

"She's okay," Brock said through the intergalactic connection. "The doctor said everything is fine. Mikayla's tired and rundown and low on vitamin D."

"That makes sense," Lachlan said, turning the information over in his mind. "Vitamin D deficiency can trigger depression in space travelers. I'll check the UV lights on the station are working correctly." Brock nodded his agreement. Either the lights they used as an equivalent for the Earth's sunshine weren't working the way they were supposed to, or there was something on the planet draining vitamin D from their bodies. Either way, Lachlan and his brothers probably hadn't been affected because of the vitamin supplement they were taking to counteract the mouse tears' effects.

"Anyway, the doctor has suggested she take vitamin supplements while she's off planet, but the good news is that she should be fine in a few days." He ran a hand through his hair and huffed out a tired breath. "But emotionally, she's still pulling away. I can feel it, Lachlan, and I don't know how to stop it. I wish you or Bryce were here. Maybe you could tell me what we're doing wrong. I feel like we're losing her."

"I doubt you're doing anything wrong," Lachlan said sympathetically. It wasn't often that Brock was unsure of himself. "Just keep her close."

Lachlan didn't voice his theory out loud for fear that it was very close to the truth. He suspected that their beautiful wife was considering leaving them partly because the female scientists seemed to undermine her confidence and partly because she was frightened to fall pregnant again. He and Mikayla had very briefly discussed trying again when they got back to Earth, but the closer that time came, the more she seemed to withdraw into herself. Of course a vitamin D deficiency would probably exacerbate those emotions.

Brock ran his hands down his face and made an obvious effort to try to pull himself together. "We're booked on the next sky-pod to California. Hopefully spending time with Tracey will help."

Lachlan nodded and went to say something when the proximity alarm started howling again. "Damn, the raiders are getting bolder and far more stupid. This is the third group today. We've started wearing protective gear just so we don't end up splattered in something unpleasant." He gave that last word a whole lot more meaning just by the way he said it.

Brock nodded, seeming in control once more and closed the connection. Lachlan had barely a moment to consider his brother's uncharacteristic behavior as he headed to the communications room to gather his equipment and find out where the raiders had landed.

* * * *

It was probably really silly considering that Mikayla had eight husbands, but arriving at Tracey's home made her feel like she finally had someone she could lean on for a little while. Her men were very supportive, but it felt awful to lean on them when it was her own fears causing the problem. It would seem, however, that the doctor's theory was proving correct because the more time she spent in the sunshine the more she felt like herself.

Tracey took one look at her and pulled Mikayla in for a hug. How she managed to get John and Brock to leave the room was a mystery, but leave they did. They hadn't left Mikayla alone for a single moment since they'd boarded the cruiser back on the jungle planet. She understood what they were doing, and she was somewhat annoyed by it, but she wouldn't give them grief for trying to help her.

"What's going on?" Tracey asked immediately.

Mikayla tried to smile reassuringly, but when Tracey gave her a knowing look, she said, "Just working through some stuff in my head."

"Stuff?" Tracey asked. "What sort of stuff?"

"I'm just being silly. Everything's okay. I'm fine really."

"I know you," Tracey said with a wag of her finger, "you're not fine, and the last thing you would've done is lean on those husbands of yours, so explain to me what this stuff is about and we can work through it together." Mikayla smiled slightly. Yes, Tracey did know her. She knew how Mikayla sometimes struggled to retain her sense of self when faced with eight very large men with personalities to match. She loved them dearly, desperately even, but it would be very easy to stop being herself and become the helpless, pathetic female she'd always despised. As much as she enjoyed their coddling, there had to be a limit.

"So talk to me, Mikayla?" Tracey asked slowly as if she was measuring every word. "Is this about getting pregnant again?"

Mikayla shrugged, trying to hide just how scared she felt. When she'd learned she was pregnant, she'd been so excited, but that high had dived to a new terrifying low when she'd miscarried. Time hadn't made things less painful. In fact, the passage of time had just made the memories more powerful. She closed her eyes as if by admitting the truth without seeing anything it would somehow make it less damning.

"I don't think I can go through it again," she said, nearly whispering. The tears leaked out of her closed eyes and Tracey made a sympathetic noise.

"Do your husbands know how you feel?"

Mikayla shook her head but added, "I think they suspect it, though."

"Good," Tracey said, sounding for all the world like an avenging angel. "It'll save me time if I don't have to kick their asses. You need time to heal—emotionally as well as physically. Take a year or two off from planning a family. Just enjoy being married and forget about babies for a while."

Mikayla nodded, feeling a guilty relief that someone else shared her opinion. She kept telling herself it was silly to be reacting the way she was, but she just couldn't shake the fear. And of course that niggling doubt of her own worth as a woman reared its ugly head, and she once again found herself wondering if her husbands would be better off without her as their wife. What if it happened again? What if she was never able to give them children? Maybe if she got out of the way, they could find several wives between them and have a whole houseful of kids within a couple years.

"I should let them go," she said, shaking her head sadly, "but I'm such a coward. I don't want to live without them." She whispered the words even as she meant to hide the thoughts.

"No," Tracey said, sounding horrified. "You love those men, and they love you." Tracey glanced at the closed door, and Mikayla found herself kind of hoping that her men were listening. Maybe if they knew she was willing to step aside, they'd take the hard steps for her.

"You listen to me Mikayla Davidson," Tracey said angrily. "Not one of those men will ever look to replace you. They love you with everything in them. I may not have met Bryce face-to-face, but if he's as much like Matt as you've told me, he'll never let you go either. You're it. You're the one for all of them." She took a deep breath, grabbed both of Mikayla's hands, and squeezed reassuringly. "They will love you until the end of time whether you stay with them or not. Don't you dare go doing something stupid out of misdirected loyalty. All you will do is make yourself and eight wonderful men miserable."

Mikayla nodded. Her heart squeezed at the thought of hurting her guys, but she worried that she'd never find the courage to try to become pregnant again. She feared that years into the future, when they were old and gray and there weren't any Davidson children to carry on the family name, her husbands would grow to resent her.

"John is renegotiating the mining survey contract, so we'll see what happens before I make any firm decisions."

Tracey still looked worried, but she nodded once as if she sensed Mikayla couldn't take much more and then changed the subject.

They spent some time talking about day to day stuff, catching up on each other's lives. By the time Mikayla finished telling Tracey about the mating musk of the mouse tears and the interesting effects it had on the human male population, they were practically giggling like a couple of schoolgirls.

"Thank God we landed on the planet at the beginning of mating season. The stuff seems far more potent now."

Tracey waggled her eyebrows suggestively, and Mikayla laughed again. "Ah, no. If it's potent enough to have raiders rubbing against trees, I don't even want to think about what eight husbands would be *up* for."

They giggled again at Mikayla's double entendre. A moment later, Rick came through the front door. He was dressed in his police uniform and smiling widely. "That," he said as he stepped toward Tracey, "is a very lovely sound to come home to." Rick kissed his wife tenderly and then turned to Mikayla with a broad smile. "So did you get out without your husbands, or are they lurking on the other side of the door?"

"Other side of the door," Mikayla said, feeling happier than she had in months. Things weren't perfect, and she still had a lot of emotions to work through, but at least she had a clearer outlook. How could she have forgotten how much her husbands loved her?

Chapter Four

"Shit, get Mikayla out of here." John's whispered order had Brock going immediately to red alert. They were in the middle of New York standing out the front of their lawyer's offices. What the hell could be so dangerous? "That's Peter's ex," John growled as he moved to intercept the woman. She'd spotted Mikayla and was marching in her direction.

Brock grabbed Mikayla, turned her around, and headed into the nearest dress shop. Hopefully, she hadn't seen Jessie Evans. The woman was toxic. Even after she'd had a breakdown in open court, she'd continued to harass Peter via intergalactic messages. Her last had almost been comical. She was sorry—yeah, right. She still loved him—still? She would do anything to win him back—never going to happen.

Without the threat of further legal action, Peter, Mikayla, and all the brothers had simply ignored Jessie's ever increasing messages. They would probably need to file for a restraining order before long, but with the distance between Earth and the jungle planet, they'd felt safe. Too bad they hadn't considered having the worst luck in history by running into the woman in a crowded city on a planet that few knew they were visiting.

"What's going on?" Mikayla asked, sounding a little alarmed. He considered lying, but she hadn't been happy about them keeping her in the dark over Peter's legal battle, so he caved and told the truth.

"Jessie Evans is just outside. John is making sure that she knows to send any further communications via our lawyers." Mikayla nodded, but he could see her curiosity and concern. "Please just let

John handle it this time." Mikayla hadn't been herself lately. The last thing she needed was to be called all sorts of nasty names by a woman with no class and zero sympathy for others.

"Okay," Mikayla said, moving to look at some of the clothes. Stunned to near speechlessness, Brock opened and closed his mouth several times. He'd at least expected to have to argue a little.

Mikayla tried on three dresses before John joined them in the clothing store. He looked pale, so it was a pretty good guess that whatever Jessie had said wasn't good. He wanted to ask for a word by word accounting but didn't want to upset Mikayla, so he stayed quiet. Mikayla saw John and stepped into his embrace for a moment.

"Thanks," she said and then pressed a quick kiss to his mouth. "I just don't have the energy to deal with that woman right now." He nodded, looking surprised by her attitude, and then quickly changed the subject.

"So how many dresses should we buy for our lovely wife?" he asked Brock.

"I'm thinking at least a dozen." She smiled but shook her head.

"Ten?" John asked hopefully.

"Two," she said with a big grin. It was so wonderful to see her smile that Brock didn't even care that she refused to let them spoil her. "And maybe another bra," she said, digging her fingers into her ribs and adjusting the support garment yet again. At home, the only time she wore one was when the female scientists came to visit, and thankfully that was a very rare occurrence.

All of his brothers preferred her breasts unbound, but as she led them into the undergarments section, wicked ideas swirled through Brock's head. There were so many sexy things to choose from. She saw the look on his face and laughed happily.

"And how long do you think they'd stay on?" she teased.

"Not the point, baby girl," he said as he pushed several different styles into her hands. "I think you need to try these on." She glanced at the tags, blanched at the price, and went to put them back. "That wasn't a request, baby girl."

She smiled, rolled her eyes like a very naughty sub, and moved toward the fitting room. As soon as she was out of earshot, Brock turned to John. The man didn't need any prompting.

"She wants a meeting with Mikayla. Says she wants to apologize."

"You told her to go to hell, right?"

"Damn straight," John said. "Apart from the fact I don't believe a word of what she says, she was just a little too excited to see Mikayla. We should get out of New York as quickly as possible."

"Agreed." Brock checked the time. "Your appointment is in fifteen minutes. Mikayla and I will wait in the reception area. I was going to take her shopping, but with that bitch hanging around, I don't want to chance it."

"Maybe we should bring her into the meeting," John said casually, maybe a little too casually. When he saw Brock's expression, he started to explain. "She's got a quick intellect and a good mind for business. I think it would help her to be more involved." Brock just stared at his brother for a few moments. There was no doubt Mikayla was intelligent, and she'd proved she could cope with pressure when she'd been thrust into the middle of Peter's court case, but did she really need the stress of the family business when she'd had so much to cope with lately?

John must've interpreted his hesitation correctly because he added, "I think she needs to feel part of the business as well as part of the family."

Brock nodded slowly. He didn't want Mikayla stressing over the family business as well as her family, but he could see John's wisdom. It wouldn't really hurt for her to feel more involved in the business side. They'd both heard her whispered confession to Tracey, and it had taken every ounce of strength not to burst through the door and yell at her for her foolish assumptions. Only Tracey's fierce rebuttal had calmed his shrieking nerves. He couldn't lose Mikayla. He wouldn't allow it.

* * * *

John looked at his brother and wished he could read minds. Brock was always so controlled that even when he was on the verge of losing it, he still seemed calm. Ever since overhearing the conversation they should not have been listening to, John had wondered how to give Mikayla another reason for staying with them. Giving her a more personal stake in the family business was probably a little selfish in some ways—it was one more reason for her to hesitate if she chose to leave them—but John felt the good outweighed the bad in this case.

Before they could go into more detail, Mikayla stepped out of the fitting room and headed back to them. She went to put several of the outfits back on the rack, but Brock stopped her.

"They're uncomfortable," she said as she tried again to hang them back where they belonged.

"Uncomfortable how?" Brock asked with a broad smile.

"Uncomfortable as in I would rather wear a suit of armor."

"Perfect." Brock grinned as he snatched the outfits away from her. "John and I want a fashion show tonight. You can point out the places these outfits are making uncomfortable, and we'll kiss them all better."

She smiled and threw her hands in the air, but John didn't miss the way her eyes darkened with arousal or the way she moved her legs as if to quell the tingling between them. It was almost like the real Mikayla was emerging once more. It was only now when she was starting to be herself again that he realized just how much she'd withdrawn in the last six months. Taking a year off even thinking about baby making, per Tracey's suggestion, was a great idea. But how could they convince Mikayla without letting on that they'd heard the conversation?

The meeting with their lawyer went better than expected. Mikayla bought up a few points that John hadn't even considered, and their lawyer had seemed fairly confident he could convince the mining company that the contract was void due to the current working conditions. Their lawyer also made a few discreet enquiries about the medical consortium and discovered that they had indeed been relying on Lachlan's war hero status to keep their staff safe instead of hiring security of their own. Their lawyer had every intention of playing the two companies against each other and winning a favorable outcome for the Davidson family.

"We'll be in California for another week," Brock said to their lawyer as they left the office. "Then we're planning to head home, hopefully with a new security team on board."

"Just make sure they're all female," the lawyer said with a grim smile. "I don't even want to think about the legal ramifications of employees getting injured humping trees." The man shuddered, not the slightest trace of humor in his voice. John wanted to laugh at the image the lawyer conjured but managed to keep the urge under control and nodded instead.

Brock was already whispering in Mikayla's ear by the time they reached the elevator. Her legs wobbled as they stepped into the empty compartment, and Brock wasted no time pressing her between her two husbands.

"Baby girl," he whispered quietly. "John and I are going to remind you of all the reasons you married us."

She nodded and looked over her shoulder to give John a soft smile. Every instinct he owned screamed at him to urge her to her knees and ram his cock deep into her heavenly mouth. She pressed back against him as his dick grew against her ass cheeks. "I know what you're thinking," she said in a voice full of promise. "You, too," she said to Brock.

The walk back to their hotel seemed to take forever. Desperate to make love to his wife, John lifted her in his arms and carried her the last few hundred feet. By the time they made it to their room, his cock was nearly hard enough to tear through the material of his jeans.

"Hands and knees," Brock said as soon as the door closed.

Mikayla dropped to all fours immediately, a soft smile gracing her beautiful lips—lips John planned to have wrapped around his cock any moment.

Brock nodded as John stripped off his clothes and knelt in front of Mikayla. She licked his cock as soon as he was close enough, and the unexpected caress sent his blood pressure soaring. It had been so long since they'd been together intimately that he wasn't sure he would last through the first hard suck on his aching flesh.

Naked, Brock knelt behind Mikayla, lifted her dress over her hips and pulled her panties halfway down her thighs. The first slap took John by surprise. Again and again Brock's large hand landed on Mikayla's ass. "Why are you being punished, baby girl?"

She shook her head, her uncertain gaze meeting John's own confused expression. Punished?

"This is for not talking to us." Brock slapped her again, even harder. "This is for not trusting us enough to tell us how you felt." The slaps didn't abate, and for a moment John wondered whether he should intervene. Brock seemed angrier than John had ever seen him. "And this is for doubting that we love you."

Tears flowed freely from Mikayla's eyes, but she didn't protest. Brock rubbed his hand soothingly over her reddened flesh. "Don't leave me, baby girl," he said, sounding on the verge of tears himself.

Mikayla's expression showed her own concern, but then Brock did something else, and she closed her eyes for a moment and moaned loudly. As the heat from Brock's spanking finally morphed into desire, Mikayla's eyes darkened with arousal and a sensual smile graced her face. John couldn't resist rubbing his cock gently against her lips. Without warning, she greedily sucked him into her mouth.

She worked his cock frantically, sucking harder as she shook with her own orgasm and Brock thrust into her from behind. The hard, urgent pace meant John's cock slid deeper down her throat every time Brock thrust into her pussy. She practically screamed around his erection as her whole body shook with release. John couldn't hold back his own orgasm any longer. Heat boiled in his groin, and then cum burst from his cock, filling her mouth, splashing her throat with his seed.

She swallowed convulsively, refusing to let him pull away. He caressed her hair and face as Brock finally stopped thrusting into her and held still. Brock leaned over, still lodged in her pussy, and kissed the back of her neck. "I love you, Mikayla," he said very seriously. "Please don't ever forget that."

Mikayla finally released the suction she had on John's cock and looked over her shoulder to Brock. John couldn't quite believe the hurt he read on Brock's face and again wondered if he should intervene. But Mikayla knew exactly what to say.

"I'm sorry, Master."

With a stifled groan, Brock wrapped his arms around her and rolled them both onto their sides on the floor. Still intimately joined, he closed his eyes and held his wife like she was the only anchor in his suddenly rocky world. John felt a touch of embarrassment for having witnessed something so intensely private. Brock had never shown any weakness in front of his younger brothers, and to witness it firsthand was somewhat humbling.

Both Lachlan and Brock always seemed like the responsible older brothers. Always in control, always doing the right thing, making the hard decisions, and it was easy to forget that they were human with the same frail emotions as the rest of them.

John moved away, quietly hoping Mikayla could reassure his brother that she had no intention of leaving.

Chapter Five

Emotion sat like a heavy ball in her stomach. She'd been so caught up in her own misery she hadn't even noticed how difficult it had been for Brock to deal with everything that had been happening.

Caught in the vise-like grip of his arms, she lay quietly and accepted his intense embrace. She'd seen the concern on John's face as he'd left the room, and she'd felt even more wretched knowing that she'd let her husbands down.

"I'm sorry, Brock," she managed to whisper. "I didn't mean to hurt you. Please forgive me."

"I forgive you, baby girl, but you need to promise to be honest with me, with all of us, from now on. If you have a problem, you need to discuss it with your husbands, not bottle it inside."

She nodded again, struggling to keep the tears at bay.

"Good girl," he said, his hand stroking up and down her arm, over her hip, and to the edges of her sore bottom. "Let's get cleaned up. I need to take care of your ass or you won't sit comfortably for a week."

"Maybe that's a good thing," she said, still feeling remorse for what she'd put him through. "It might remind me not to keep secrets."

He laughed quietly. "That it might," then added thoughtfully, "but it will also stop me from spanking you again this week, and I suspect that you have quite a few spankings coming your way, baby girl. It's been a long time since I got to play with my sub properly."

Brock carefully rolled away from her, got to his feet, and lifted her into his arms. "Tomorrow," he said conversationally, "we'll go to California and visit Tracey and her husbands for a while. Then John and I are going to lock you in our hotel room and keep you naked for five days straight."

* * * *

Lachlan cursed at the latest proximity alarm. Now the bastards were landing in the dark as well. It didn't matter that he wasn't asleep or that they had night-vision equipment. It still pissed him off that they'd even think of trespassing in the middle of the fucking night.

He was halfway to the communications room when Ryan, Ty, and Bryce met him in the hallway. "We've got this one," Ty said with his usual trademark smile. "You can answer the subspace communicator."

Now that he was close enough, Lachlan could hear the insistent buzzing noise. He glanced back at his brothers, but they were almost at the end of the hall before it occurred to Lachlan that if it had been Mikayla, they wouldn't have been so keen to hand over the task.

When he saw the ID code, he wanted to run in the opposite direction, too. As much as he loved his mother, she could be a royal pain in the ass when something was on her mind.

"Hi, Mom," he said, trying not to sound anything but neutral. The woman's talent for reading body language was as freaky as his own, and he knew any sign of weakness would lead to a lecture on whatever subject took her fancy.

"Lachlan, you look tired," she began without preamble. He tried not to roll his eyes in irritation. Their parents were all well aware of the situation they were dealing with, so his mom should know exactly why he seemed tired.

"What's up, Mom?" he asked, trying not to sound exasperated. If she'd just get to the point, he'd be able to deal with whatever disaster she wanted him to handle and then he could go back to bed.

"I met a lovely young lady today," she said casually. She'd started many a conversation with the exact same opening line when she'd been trying to set him up on a date. Had she forgotten he was married now? He raised an eyebrow, letting his irritation leak into his body language. She noticed.

"Well anyway, she said she was Peter's fiancée and—"

Lachlan cut off her words. "Is she still there?"

His mother looked a little alarmed at his vehemence but shook her head. "We just wondered what was going on. Your fathers reckon Peter would never marry anyone besides Mikayla, but Sandra and I were wondering if maybe you'd finally reconsidered. I mean, with Mikayla's miscarriage, it makes sense that you would take on a few extra wives to complete your family."

She took a deep breath but started talking again before Lachlan could get his temper under control enough to set his mother straight. "You know, none of you are getting any younger, and Sandra and I didn't birth eight sons between us just to end up with no grandchildren." She folded her arms, and he sensed her deliberate attempt to intimidate him into silence. It may have worked when he was seven, but she seemed to have forgotten he was a grown man.

"First of all," he said, but she went to cut him off. He widened his stance, crossed his arms, and lowered his voice. He loved the woman dearly, but she sure could push his buttons. "First of all," he repeated, "Jessie Evans is dangerous. She is not engaged to Peter, and the last time Peter saw her was in court as she tried to sue us for everything we've got." His mother opened her mouth, but he spoke over her before she could get the first word out. "Secondly, you are very lucky that Mikayla didn't overhear that rant. If I ever hear you talk so callously about her miscarriage again, I will refuse to take your calls. Are we clear?"

His mother nodded but looked really shocked at his harsh words. A moment later her expression turned to one of remorse as if she'd just realized what she'd said. "Oh, honey, I'm sorry. I didn't mean it the way it came out. You know we love Mikayla. It's just that we'd love grandchildren too, and with all eight of you married to the same woman..." Her words trailed off as she realized she was digging herself back into the same hole.

"Mom," Lachlan said, trying to see the argument from all angles, "we will have children. If Mikayla can't carry them herself, we'll work something out. Please just let it go for now."

"O...okay," she said, seeming uncharacteristically unsure of herself. "But what should we do if Jessie turns up again?"

"Call the police and have her arrested. I'm going to contact our lawyer and get a restraining order in place. Jessie Evans has gone far enough."

His mother nodded, but she still seemed hesitant.

"I'll let you know if she comes back."

Lachlan nodded, said his goodbyes, and then leaned his elbows on the desk. He scrubbed a hand over his face and tried not to think about how devastated Mikayla would've been if she'd overheard that conversation. For the first time since she'd left with Brock and John, Lachlan was very glad she wasn't close by.

He had no idea how long he sat there contemplating the situation, but he nearly jumped a foot in the air when he heard his brothers' laughter as they came in through the security door at the front of the building. Shaken by his own uncharacteristic behavior, he went to meet them and get a run-down on what had happened with this group of raiders.

* * * *

She'd very literally been naked for three days straight, and she was beginning to think the whole wearing clothes thing was overrated. Any time the inclination took them, Brock and John turned to her with a wicked grin and moments later she was either screaming in orgasm or begging for one.

Brock had stayed true to his word and spanked her more than once. But right now she had a plug up her ass big enough to prepare her for one of their cocks. It had been so long since she'd had anal sex with any of her men that Brock had insisted they take time to prepare her. Of course both Brock and John had "inspected" the damn thing several times in the last half hour, and thanks to their attentions she'd been on the verge of explosive orgasm the whole time.

Frustrated and needy, she dropped her hand to her clit just wanting to take the edge off, but John saw her, nodded at Brock, and the next thing she knew she was ass up face down over the sofa with her arms stretched out in front of her. She tried to wiggle so that she could press her clit against just about anything, but they held her trapped.

Brock tapped the end of the plug, and liquid warmth burst through her abdomen. He pulled it out a little way and then pushed it back in, then did it again and again, slowly fucking her with the plug. She moaned, but the sound was quickly stopped by John's cock. He wrapped her arms around his hips and stepped closer, forcing his cock deeper. He held her still, fucking her mouth in the same slow, lazy rhythm Brock was using.

She growled her irritation, but John managed to extricate his cock despite her desperate sucking and near death grip on his thighs. He stepped away.

"Naughty subs don't get rewards," Brock warned as he pushed the plug back into place.

"I'll be good," she promised but then ruined it by adding in a sexy voice, "very, very good." John laughed, and Brock landed a slap on her ass. A minute later, she found herself sitting on the most uncomfortable chair in the history of uncomfortable chairs, her hands secured behind her back, her legs tied open, and her clit and ass throbbing.

She growled when Brock turned back to his book and caressed her knee absently. "Be a good sub and I won't use the O-ring." Damn, she was frustrated enough that even the thing she despised the most didn't seem worse than sitting on this chair, on the verge of orgasm, waiting for her husbands to let her come.

"O-ring?" John asked curiously. Brock pulled the despised mouth piece from his pocket and Mikayla nearly choked on how close she'd come to actually wearing the damn thing. She shut her mouth, grinding her teeth together just in case Brock changed his mind.

John looked more than a little curious, and she really, really wanted to tell him not even to think about it. But of course talking now would give Brock the perfect excuse to put the damn thing on her, so she kept quiet and dropped her head down to avoid making demands with her eyes.

"Good girl," Brock said, obviously aware of her reaction.

They made her wait, but eventually John knelt at her feet and touched her intimately with his tongue. She moaned at the delicious sensation, nearly crying with relief when Brock loosened the straps on her legs and John pulled her pussy closer to his mouth.

Brock stood behind her, playing with her aching nipples as he watched his brother bring her to the brink of orgasm. Her entire body shook, her breathing labored, her back arched, her toes curled, but then John pulled away. She wanted to scream at them, but she bit her tongue because Brock had left that damn O-ring right in her line of vision.

With her arms still secured behind her back, she could only wait helplessly, hopefully begging them with her body without demanding enough to earn the gag.

"Good girl," Brock said again as he soothed her hair away from her eyes. "Good subs get rewarded." She tried to hide her relief, but he saw it anyway and ran a soothing hand over her chest and shoulders. "Stand up." She shuffled to the edge of the seat, grateful to feel Brock's steadying hand between her shoulder blades. John urged her onto her knees and then eased her forward, lowering her head and shoulders to the floor. He released her wrists from their bindings, helped her move her arms to a more comfortable position, and massaged the tired muscles.

Brock removed the butt plug and left the room for a few moments. When he came back, she could clearly hear the sound of lube as he slicked his cock. The blunt head pressed against her anus, and she eagerly pressed back against him. He slapped her thigh, ordered her to stay still, and then eased into her back passage. She panted as the delicious sting wound dark desire through her. He fucked her carefully, like she was fragile, and she wanted to growl at the slow burn, but when he pulled from her completely, she just wanted to cry.

He moved to the edge of the sofa and lay back. John lifted her off the floor and carried her over to Brock. He arranged her over Brock with her back to his chest. John pushed her knees almost to her shoulders and held her there as Brock worked his cock back into her ass. She sighed with relief as John pushed her legs wide and fit his cock against her pussy.

Their movements started awkwardly, but they soon found a rhythm and fucked her like she hadn't been fucked in months. Over and over, harder, deeper, each of her men made love to her like she was the only woman in the universe.

She cried out as Brock grabbed her nipples roughly, twisting the sensitive nubs until she melted around the pleasure. He lowered one hand to her clit, and she was lost.

Heat burst through her abdomen, the rocking-rolling sensation of having them both inside her while her body went into meltdown, stealing her voice, stealing her breath, stealing her sanity. She screamed as every muscle shook with release.

Vaguely aware of them both coming at the same time, Mikayla closed her eyes and thanked the heavens for her amazing men. John leaned over to kiss her softly as Brock shifted to nibble on her earlobe.

Exhausted, she closed her eyes.

* * * *

"She's asleep," John said, feeling pretty good about the whole fucking-their-wife-into-unconsciousness thing. It was stupid and macho bullshit, but he couldn't quite convince himself not to be so satisfied.

"Go get cleaned up," Brock said. "I'll stay here."

John laughed at Brock's obvious contentment, and then pulled his softening cock out of Mikayla's heavenly warmth. She was achingly beautiful like this. She lay sprawled across Brock's big body, her legs open, her face relaxed in sleep, and John couldn't think of any place he'd rather be.

But the shower beckoned, and the sooner he got cleaned up, the sooner he could hold Mikayla for the rest of the night. The communicator buzzed before he could get three steps, so he turned and answered the damn thing. Luckily it was Lachlan. Anyone else might've been shocked by him answering the sub-space communicator naked as a jaybird.

"We have a problem," Lachlan said immediately. "Where's Mikayla?"

"Asleep," John answered, feeling a little irritated. Did Lachlan think he wasn't looking after their wife?

"Good, but grab a headset," Lachlan ordered. Peeved at his brother's highhanded attitude, John did as ordered only because he was concerned for his wife. If Lachlan didn't want Mikayla to hear, then it was a solid bet that it wasn't good news. As soon as he had the headset in place, he nodded for Lachlan to continue.

"A few days ago Jessie Evans introduced herself to our parents as Peter's fiancée. I set them straight, but today she arrived with a handful of papers claiming that Mikayla isn't really Mikayla Noone. Mom sent them to our lawyer, and he says the papers look legitimate enough. Bryce put a call in to some old friends, and we're trying to verify the information."

John wanted to yell at Lachlan for being fool enough to believe anything provided by Jessie Evans, but he didn't want to risk waking Mikayla, so he ground his teeth together and nodded instead.

"Jessie is claiming that none of our marriages to Mikayla are genuine and that we provided fraudulent information to the courts." Fuck. The woman wasn't satisfied with trying to take their money and assets. Now she was trying to throw their asses in jail as well.

John nodded again, this time too worried he wouldn't be able to control his temper if he so much as opened his mouth.

"I think," Lachlan continued, "that there is a logical explanation. We just have to find it." John nodded in agreement and moved to take the ear piece off. Twelve months ago, if Mikayla had woken and found them talking on the communicator in complete silence, she wouldn't have let up until he'd relayed the conversation word for word. He wasn't so sure her reaction would be the same at the moment, but he didn't want to risk it.

Swallowing down his anger, John finally managed to speak in a level voice.

"We need to see the doctor again day after tomorrow, and then we were planning to head back to home."

Lachlan nodded, relief obvious on his face. "Good," he said, "we'll hire female security staff as soon as we can, but with the vitamin supplement, we should at least be able to protect Mikayla if things get out of hand."

"I'll let you know when we're leaving," John said carefully, hopefully giving Lachlan the message not to call while Mikayla was around. Jessie Evans had already done enough damage, and until they knew what the hell was going on, he'd rather Mikayla not be involved. Considering the way she'd reacted when Brock had basically hidden her in the clothing store while John dealt with Jessie's unexpected appearance, he felt fully justified in protecting her this way. She'd been angry when they'd hidden the original court case from her, but that was before she'd had several months of doubting herself. She was just beginning to find her true self again, and John was determined to give her time. They'd explain it all later, hopefully when it was all sorted out.

Chapter Six

"Welcome home, little one," Lachlan said as he pulled her into his embrace. "I've missed you."

She smiled happily and very nearly bounced from husband to husband as she greeted them all after stepping off the cruiser. She looked happier than she had in months, and Lachlan smiled gratefully at Brock and John. Whatever they'd said or done had worked. She was back to being the woman they'd married, not the stressed, timid woman she'd become in the past few months.

Ryan and Ty wrapped themselves around Mikayla and did their usual disappearing act. Lachlan smiled. Hopefully, Mikayla had gotten some sleep on their trip because she wasn't going to get any with those two. She waved over her head, obviously more than happy to go along with the twin's plans.

* * * *

Mikayla giggled happily as Ryan and Ty rushed her from the room. She suspected that the others were merely waiting for her to get out of earshot before they discussed their trip and her reactions in minute detail. She loved that they cared so much, but even now, when she knew that most of her emotional issues and concerns had been blown out of proportion by a lack of vitamin D, she couldn't help worrying that she wasn't the woman they needed.

Surely they deserved a woman braver than her. She'd never considered herself a coward before, but everyone had a breaking point. Maybe she'd found hers. Put simply, the thought of becoming pregnant again filled her with mind-numbing dread. Somehow, in her head, pregnancy had become synonymous with fear and anguish, not the beginning of a new life. Even knowing on an intellectual level that her anxiety was higher than the situation warranted still didn't give her the ability to overcome it. She just hoped she could hide it long enough from her husbands to get over the damn problem.

Finally reaching Ryan and Ty's quarters, the twins wasted no time in getting all three of them naked. Hands roamed over every inch of her skin, relearning her shape, igniting the flames of her arousal. She moaned as Ryan took a nipple in his mouth and Ty stroked a hand over her already dripping pussy.

"We missed you, darlin'," Ty said in between soft kisses and stinging little bites on the back of her neck. She moaned as Ryan bit down on the nipple he held captive and then swirled his tongue around and around the aching nub.

"I missed you, too," she managed to gasp out.

"Can't wait," Ryan said as Ty lifted her up and Ryan grabbed her knees, encouraging her to wrap her legs around his waist. His hard cock pressed against her, sliding into her pussy slowly as Ty dripped lube against her ass. Incredible tingling sensations skittered all over her as Ty finally pushed his cock into her back passage.

They stayed that way, just breathing, Mikayla simply enjoying the feeling of being one with her men. Gentle kisses and soft sighs filled the moments, but then Mikayla's muscles pulsed of their own volition, and her men began to move.

In and out, harder, deeper, but in slow rhythm like they were savoring every sweet stroke. Mikayla could feel her orgasm building rapidly. Ryan and Ty started moving faster, their coordination perfect as they built the speed, the motion, the friction. Mikayla ground her teeth, trying to hold back her climax, but then Ryan whispered three little words and she was lost.

Every nerve ending tingled as energy exploded outward. She held onto Ryan, crying out as orgasm overwhelmed her and her men's movements faltered. They held her tight, their breathing rapid as she pulsed around their cocks, dragging their climaxes from them.

"I love you, too," she managed to whisper in response to Ryan's words.

Swallowing hard, she held back the tears that threatened. It was so silly to feel this way when her men so obviously loved her, but she couldn't hold back the worry that maybe she didn't deserve them.

"Shower time," Ryan said happily. A moment later, Ty moved away from her, and Ryan, still intimately joined with her legs around his waist, carried her into the bathroom. By the time they finished "cleaning" her, she was so exhausted that she had no more time to worry. She slept soundly for the first time in a long time.

* * * *

Finally able to talk without fear of Mikayla overhearing, John and Brock filled their brothers in on what they'd learned in their limited amount of investigating while on Earth.

Basically, Mikayla Noone hadn't been born.

She existed. She had social security records, job and travel history, and taxation records, but they only went back to her eighteenth birthday. Everything before that was a blank. No school or medical records could be located. It was possible that she'd been born off-world, but those records were always transferred to the central human database, so there should've at least been some trace of what Mikayla Noone did or where she'd been before she'd suddenly appeared at age eighteen.

The momentary uncomfortable thought that Mikayla wasn't human flitted through John's head. But he quickly dismissed it.

Of course, he knew that none of his brothers would love Mikayla any less if she wasn't human—they weren't that narrow-minded—but there were few species compatible with humans in a reproductive sense. The brief moment of anger that she might've been lying to them quickly melted into guilt for not trusting his wife.

"So now what?" Peter asked, looking about as confused as John felt. "If Jessie can get this information in front of a judge, the last verdict is liable to be overturned. I really, really don't want Mikayla to have to go through that again. Surely Jessie would find a way around the eighth brother issue this time.

"I guess we need to ask her," Brock said. He didn't look happy about it, but did they really have a choice?

"No," Peter said stubbornly. "We'll figure it out without upsetting Mikayla."

"Fine," John said, feeling caught between protecting the woman they loved and needing to know the truth. "We won't ask her unless Jessie manages to get a court date before we can figure it out."

His brothers nodded in agreement.

* * * *

"Time to feed you," Ryan said as he rolled off the bed and offered Mikayla a hand up.

"What time is it?" she asked, still feeling very relaxed and lethargic.

"Dinner time," Ty said with a wink. "Although considering that it's Peter's turn to cook, we're considering renaming it to 'inedible, jaw-breaking, unidentifiable-goo-on-a-plate' time."

She giggled quietly but didn't say a word. As much as she loved him, Peter really was an awful cook, and she sincerely hoped there never came a day when they had to rely on his culinary skills to keep them alive.

Mikayla barely made it to her feet before Ty lifted her into his arms and carried her into the bathroom. "I missed you, darlin'," he said as he lowered her to sit on the vanity while Ryan adjusted the water temperature in the shower.

"I missed you, too, but didn't we already have a shower?"

"That one didn't count," Ty said as he pulled her close and kissed her breathless.

When she could finally get her voice working, she nodded in agreement. Was there such thing as too clean?

"Anything interesting happen while I was away?" she asked, as Ryan fiddled with the water pressure and Ty gathered some towels.

"Not really," Ryan said in a suspiciously neutral tone. She glared at him a moment before turning his answer into a question.

"Not really?" she asked, waiting for one of them to expand on the non-answer.

"Well," Ty said, shrugging casually, "we did have to untangle a raider who got stuck in a tree." Almost as if he was warming to the diversionary story, he smiled and began to fill in details. Mikayla winced when she heard what part of the poor man had been held captive by a tree knot.

"Anything else?" Mikayla asked when Ty finally finished his story.

"I wonder if the others would notice if I kept you in my bed all week," Ty said, obviously avoiding answering her question. She kissed him, ready to demand a real answer, but then reality intruded, and she wondered if she really wanted to know. Uncomfortable with the self-revelation, she tried not to overthink it as she took the coward's way out and stuck with the current topic.

"As much as I love the idea, I'm certain that your brothers would not only notice but probably be a tad upset." Completely pissed would be closer to the mark, but Ryan and Ty managed to look crestfallen all the same. "Besides," she added, trying to ignore their feigned miserable expressions. "I'll be back in the lab tomorrow." They both brightened considerably.

"That's true," Ryan said with a wicked expression, "we'll need to find time for several coffee breaks." Mikayla rolled her eyes at his lascivious expression and waggling eyebrows.

"True," she said, already looking forward to doing some actual work tomorrow,

She laughed happily as Ty lifted her and the three of them managed to step into the shower stall together. Within moments, she was on the verge of climax, and by the time they'd finished making love to her again, they were very late for dinner.

* * * *

"They're hiding something from me," Mikayla said to Tracey over the subspace communicator several days later.

"Maybe it was just them excited for you to be back," she said thoughtfully, "but knowing how much they worry about you, I think you're right. It's probably more than that."

Mikayla nodded as she slid onto the chair in front of the screen. "Trouble is I don't think I want to know."

"Mikayla," Tracey said, sounding concerned. "Do you have any idea what it could be about?"

"Jessie Evans."

"Seriously? I thought the courts settled that already."

"So did I," Mikayla said, "but we ran into her in New York and Brock and John hid me in a clothing store, and I sort of…well I sort of let them."

Tracey looked at her as if she'd grown a second head.

"I know," Mikayla said in answer to the unasked question, "but I was just feeling so worn out, and it seemed easier to let them take care of me than face whatever vitriol that woman wanted to hurl."

Tracey leaned back in her chair and watched Mikayla for a moment. "I'll accept that. You were tired and sad, but what's your excuse now?"

Mikayla grimaced at Tracey's easy summation of her current predicament. How many times had she explained her need to retain her independence amid eight husbands? Yes, she'd been tired and unhappy, but that wasn't the case anymore, and she really didn't have any excuse for remaining in the dark.

"I guess I need to go hunt down some answers," she said, feeling a rueful smile spread across her face.

"Now that's the Mikayla I know."

Mikayla waved to her friend as she leaned over to close the connection. "Thanks for reminding me."

Chapter Seven

She marched into his office just the way she used to. Lachlan sat back in his chair and threaded his fingers together as he waited for her to say what was on her mind. She looked beautiful. The fear and stress she'd struggled with was gone and the vibrant, passionate woman was back—at least for the moment.

"I need to know," she stated bluntly.

"Agreed," he said and watched as her determination morphed into delight. As much as he wanted to protect her, she had a right to know the accusations that were being launched in her direction. Knowing that she wanted to know made it so much easier to treat her the way he always had.

She crossed her arms and waited for him to explain.

"Jessie Evans is claiming that you are not Mikayla Noone." He watched her smile falter and then her face flush with anger.

"That heinous, callous bitch. I suppose she managed to figure out that Mikayla Noone wasn't my name until I turned eighteen. Did she figure out who I was? Did she fill you in on all the sordid details?"

She was shaking and looked ready to wring the woman's neck, but all Lachlan could think was how proud he was of her. Instead of letting the woman undermine her, Mikayla was ready to kick some ass.

"No, she didn't," Bryce said from the doorway. "She doesn't know your real name."

"My real name," she said, emphasizing the word "real" with an almost growl, "is Mikayla Davidson." She turned to face Bryce and Matt as they came in the room. "Before I married you my name was

Mikayla Noone. Noone as in No One. Who I was before that is none of her goddamn business."

"I totally agree," Bryce said affably. Mikayla was holding her jaw so tightly that Lachlan was beginning to fear for her teeth. "But the courts might think otherwise."

"Why?" she asked, obviously irritated beyond measure.

"Because Jessie Evans is claiming that our marriages are not legal and that we provided false information to the courts the last time."

"Oh for fuck's sake," she said, sounding completely and totally exasperated. "Jessie Evans is a fucking cow." Lachlan really wanted to spank her ass for swearing but couldn't quite wipe the broad smile off his own face. When his wife had a reason she was quite magnificent in her anger. "Call our lawyer. Tell him to contact this man," she said as she typed a name and contact details into Lachlan's data tablet. "He will confirm that my details are sealed and none of Jessie Evans's goddamn business."

"Okay," Lachlan said happily, "problem solved. Thanks, Mikayla."

She looked shocked by his answer. Jessie Evans deserved every harsh word that came out of Mikayla's mouth, but he was happy to let the matter simply drop now. If Mikayla was able to provide them with enough details to discredit Jessie Evans's information, then that's all he needed to know.

"You—" She cut herself off, looked between the three of them, and tried again. "You don't want an explanation?"

"Nope," Bryce said as leaned against Lachlan's desk and crossed his ankles. He was the picture of relaxation, and Lachlan grinned as Matt tried to follow his lead. Matt, however, wasn't quite as successful, and his need to always be in control reared its head.

"But if you want to tell us…" he said but trailed off when he saw Bryce's reaction. "Fine, okay, shutting up now."

Mikayla smiled at him, her anger completely gone.

"You're not going to be happy until you know," she said quietly.

Matt shook his head. "No, honey, I'm fine. I know who you are now. That's what's important."

"So you have no curiosity over what happened before I met you." Lachlan tried to hide his laugh as Mikayla looked very confused. It was obvious Matt really wanted to know.

"N–no," he lied. Mikayla half grinned, half frowned, but told him anyway.

"It's not that big a deal," she said, shrugging her shoulders. "You already know I didn't have any family before meeting you and your brothers. As a kid I was bounced around in the foster system. By the time I was sixteen, I wanted nothing more than to be in charge of my own life." She ran a hand through her hair, and Lachlan realized with a small jolt that she wasn't nearly as calm as she was pretending.

"Anyway, there aren't many jobs a sixteen-year-old can get that will pay the rent and buy food, so I fell in with a group of people who weren't exactly honest. By the time I realized what they actually were doing, I was in pretty deep." She took a big breath as if there wasn't quite enough oxygen in the air and then lounged against the wall in an obvious effort to appear calm. "So, basically, I turned state's witness, helped to prosecute the leaders, and got myself and a couple of others out of the mess we were in."

Lachlan glanced at Bryce and realized he was probably thinking the same thing he was. The level of security surrounding her new identity meant that the people she'd testified against were seriously high on the criminal food chain. The fact that Bryce hadn't been able to learn anything through official channels meant that Mikayla was probably lucky to have walked away alive. Thank God they hadn't tried Bryce's unofficial channels.

"Are you safe now?" Bryce asked. Lachlan could see the muscle ticking in Bryce's jaw and suspected he was feeling as worried as Lachlan. All the color had drained from Matt's face.

"Yes," she said reassuringly. "Even if they manage to figure out who I am, the people who went to jail because of my testimony are long dead. Do you remember the Andromedes Prison ship disaster?"

Andromedes? Hell, did he ever. While transferring notorious crime bosses, the intergalactic transport ship had been attacked and boarded by members of a major crime family. The captain had ordered the self-destruct, and the explosion had obliterated the prison ship and the ship belonging to their attackers. Passengers on a passing cruise liner had recorded the whole thing. About a year later, the prison ship's internal security images had been released on intergalactic news channels and left very little doubt as to the fate of both the prisoners and crew.

"Fuck me," Matt said on a breathless wheeze as he finally took a seat.

"Matt," she said as she moved to sit beside him. "It's okay. Even if there are any family members left, the government seized all their assets and I doubt they have enough money to worry about seeking revenge. I was a pretty small piece of the case that convicted them, and they didn't know my part in it."

"Then why take a new name? Why not go back to your old name?"

"Because it wasn't who I was anymore. Mikayla Noone might've been no one, but the memories I have of my childhood were not worth holding on to. I wanted to start anew. If I hadn't fallen for Jet's lies, I might still be Mikayla Noone, quiet, efficient administration assistant."

She smiled that hauntingly sexy smile, and Lachlan wanted nothing more than to drag her over his desk and love her until they didn't have the energy to move. "I know what you're thinking," she said to Bryce.

He laughed and asked his question anyway. "With that type of experience behind you, how did you fall for Jet's lies?"

She shrugged and tilted her head to the side. Her smile seemed a little crooked. "I guess, like a lot of people, I wanted to be loved so desperately I didn't try to look past the surface."

"And now?" Matt asked as he pulled her onto his lap.

"Now, I am loved by eight very incredible men who I know will love me regardless of my colorful past." Matt looked very relieved by her answer.

Bryce looked thoughtful for a moment and then said a little hesitantly, "I might still have the right contacts to create a background to go with the rest of you."

Mikayla smiled slightly. "Angels or devils?" she asked.

"Angels," Bryce said with a smile. "All legal and, well, sort of aboveboard, I promise you. I have a friend who creates rock-solid backgrounds for undercover cops. I'm certain he can fill in a few blanks for you."

"Okay," she said, looking more relieved than Lachlan would've expected. "Maybe if there are enough details, Jessie Evans and her bloodhounds might back off."

"It's settled then," Bryce said with a nod as he stood up. "No time like the present." He grinned as he left the room and Lachlan marveled at how easily Bryce could contain his curiosity. Despite the fact that Lachlan would deny it until his last breath, he really wanted to know Mikayla's name before she'd changed it.

She snuggled into Matt's embrace and looked more relaxed than she had in a long time.

"Why don't you two go take a nap," Lachlan said with a quick wink, partially wishing he could be there as well but also realizing that Matt needed to spend some quality time with their wife. The man still looked very pale.

Mikayla smiled at Lachlan, mouthed the words "thank you" and then whispered in Matt's ear. A smile broke across Matt's face at the same time he lifted their wife into his arms and carried her from the room. Lachlan laughed quietly as he realized the ungrateful bastard hadn't even said goodbye.

* * * *

Matt's arms trembled slightly as he held Mikayla close. He'd known she was reluctant to talk about her past, but he never would've guessed the reality. God, he wanted to lock her in his room and never let the world near her again.

They'd barely made it out of Lachlan's office when the proximity alert started shrieking once more. He could hear Lachlan cursing as he collected his weapons, and Matt got out of the way as Bryce bolted down the hall to the communications room and then came running back a moment later.

"What have we got?" Lachlan asked him.

"We've got two ships. One aft," Bryce said as he ran toward them. "One…ah…not aft?"

"Not aft?" Lachlan asked with a raised eyebrow. Bryce just shrugged. He'd spent most of his life on Earth, so it was no surprise he wasn't familiar with ship terminology.

"Stay with Mikayla," Lachlan ordered Matt.

"We'll be in the lab. I'll keep her safe." Matt promised as he put Mikayla on her feet and grabbed her hand.

Together they ran to lab and found Ryan sitting calmly reading the intergalactic news on the computer.

"Did you know," he said as they entered the room, "that the mouse tears have been declared an illegal substance?"

"What?" Mikayla and Matt asked at the same time.

"Nice of the medical consortium to tell us, huh?"

"You have got to be kidding me," Matt said, knowing he sounded completely pissed off. The only reason they were still on this strange jungle planet was because they were protecting the female scientists. If the profit—legal profit at least—had been taken out of the mouse tears equation, then it was a good bet that the medical consortium would pull their research funding. Considering their track record, it was even more likely that they would abandon their scientists right here.

"Are the girls safe?" Matt felt Mikayla bristle at his use of the term "girls," but he didn't have time to apologize. With two ships worth of raiders and probably the rest of his brothers outside trying to track them down, he felt responsible for all four women in his care.

"Ty is with them," Ryan said reassuringly. "I was talking to them when the alarm sounded."

Matt nodded, grateful that he didn't have to figure out how to keep Mikayla safe and somehow get the scientists here or Mikayla over there. Ryan seemed a little too calm and entirely engrossed with his computer until Matt realized he was monitoring the teams' movements.

Lachlan and Bryce had headed toward the larger of the two raiding vessels and John, Brock, and Peter had headed out the front door to intercept the smaller craft. Matt almost held his breath as twin images from their own satellite played on the screen.

"Oh my," Mikayla said with a stifled laugh. "You weren't kidding when you described the potency." On the screen you could very clearly see John stun two men who'd basically wrapped around each other and were pressed together like a sandwich. Matt had the fleeting hope that they were gay and then dismissed his concern just as quickly. What did he care if those two ended up having an awkward conversation? They shouldn't have been on the planet in the first place.

Lachlan and Bryce weren't so lucky. Five women had stepped off the larger ship and quickly spread out. Even on the tiny screen it was obvious that they were well armed and fully prepared to defend themselves.

"Call Bryce and Lachlan back," Matt said urgently.

"I can't," Ryan said frantically as he did something and started talking to John. Within moments Brock, Peter, and John were all headed toward Lachlan and Bryce's position. Fortunately, Lachlan and Bryce had already discovered the armed-to-the-teeth status of their newest visitors and stopped to assess the situation.

Matt could finally breathe when he saw his brothers all head back to the station without making contact with the raiders.

Within minutes they'd all gathered in the dining area, and a swift agreement followed. Only one of the female scientists, Misha, had argued to stay, but when Ryan showed her the news bulletin, she'd blanched and quickly agreed with everyone else.

Whether their contracts were void or not, none of them were willing to risk their lives any longer to stop the harvesting of what was now an illegal substance. It was like being caught in the middle of the poppy fields as a drug war broke out. None of them wanted to be the collateral damage.

"So we're all agreed." Brock glanced around the room as everyone nodded. "Okay, we need to move as much as we can into the ship part of the stations. We'll leave the rest behind for now and hope it survives until we can come back with an armed escort. Let's get this done."

Everyone scattered in different directions, and soon it was only Matt and Mikayla sitting at the table.

"Are you okay?" Matt asked his wife. She looked pale, and he knew she hated change. It wasn't until her confession about being shuffled around from foster home to foster home that he really understood her love of stability.

"I'm fine," she said absently, even though it was very obvious that she wasn't. She must've seen the incredulity on his face because she smiled and tried to be more convincing. "Really, I'm fine. I know that we're taking most of the station with us, and all of my husbands will be there. It's just that sudden change dredges up a lot of memories I'd rather forget."

Matt held her for a moment and then stood up and stepped back to see her face more clearly.

"Hopefully one day you'll share some of those memories."

"Why would you want to know?" she asked, sounding surprised that he would ask.

"Because your memories are part of who you are. Even when we convince ourselves that they can't hurt us anymore, something like this, the sudden change, comes along and throws a wrench in the works. If your husbands know what might trigger these sad memories, we can make certain that we're there to help you through them."

She smiled at him, stood, and touched his face with obvious affection. "You've got a noble streak a mile wide, haven't you? You knew in just a few moments that I was in trouble that day you met me. You'll always know when I'm feeling scared. It's just part of who you are, Matt Davidson." She stepped into his embrace and wrapped her arms around him. "In some ways, I owe you so much. If you hadn't gotten involved that first day, my life could be very different. And not in a good way." She ran her hand over the frown mark on his forehead. "But I promise I will share some memories with you soon."

Chapter Eight

After three weeks of living in cramped conditions, Mikayla was practically ready to scream. She'd finally told the rest of her husbands about her fear of becoming pregnant again, and their reactions had ranged from guilt and remorse that they'd asked her to have their children to absolute horror and anger that she would feel the need to hide her feelings from them.

Having had time to come to terms with her own emotions, she could see their reactions were born from their love and fear for her. Mikayla had spent most of the last few days trying to smooth over the upheaval and reassure her men that she wouldn't keep that sort of information from them again.

But still, a little space would be nice.

She managed to make it all the way into the kitchen only to find Ty seemed to have had the same idea. "Need some alone time?" he asked with a smile.

Mikayla nodded, feeling a little bit childish in her need to get away from men who did everything they did because they loved her.

"I can go," Ty said hesitantly. It was obvious that he'd started to prepare the evening meal, and Mikayla was more than happy for the help. Feeding herself and eight men had been a challenge. Feeding three extra women, all of whom seemed to think they were above domestic chores, took a lot of planning.

"No, that's okay," Mikayla said as she stepped to the sink and began rinsing vegetables, "we can be alone together."

Ty smiled, and Mikayla caught the first real sign that her husband was beginning to feel the strain as well. The ship only held just under half of the living space the station had in total, so they'd all had to make compromises. Add that to the fact that the medical science station-ship mysteriously hadn't started and they'd had no time to fix it before leaving the planet urgently, tempers were fraying at an alarming rate.

"Everything okay?" Mikayla asked quietly.

Ty looked at her for a moment and then blew out a big breath. "Fine," he answered, sounding rather tired. "It's been hard sharing a ship with those women. They don't seem to have any inclination to make allowances at all. The three of them have been arguing with Ryan since we left the planet." He turned and whispered conspiratorially, "I think Ryan is about ready to stun their asses. Next time they piss him off, you're liable to hear three dull thuds as they hit the ground."

Mikayla giggled a little and then placed her hand over her mouth. "I think I'd cheer if he did," she said, a little shocked at her own reaction.

Ty smiled as well, nodding his agreement. Mikayla had thought the female scientists were difficult to deal with back on the planet, but that was nothing compared to the angst they were causing now.

"I have half a mind not to feed them," she said as she went back to washing vegetables. "But it would only mean they'd have to use the kitchen to fend for themselves, and I sure don't want to be left to clean that mess up."

* * * *

Ryan saw Jacqueline come into the lab and tried to hide his irritation. Three weeks of attempting to avoid the woman in the cramped space of the ship was starting to wear on him. Unfortunately, Jacqueline had made it rather obvious that she had no respect for Mikayla, or for her marriage vows, and therefore saw him and his brothers as available rather than married men.

"Where's Bryce?" she asked in a tone that suggested she had a right to know. The woman was nothing if not direct. At first Ryan had dismissed her behavior as the quirks of her personality. A lot of scientific researchers had difficulty in a social setting, and he'd just figured she was one of them. He'd never been quite so wrong in his life.

"I'm not sure," he answered honestly. Bryce could be anywhere on the ship. It's not like they had a roster.

"What about Matt?" she asked in an imperious tone.

"Sorry," he answered, trying to remain polite but having difficulty. He breathed a silent sigh of relief when Ty came back into the lab.

"Jacqueline? Anything I can help you with?" Ty asked as he walked past her, heading back to his desk.

"Call Bryce and Matt for me," she said in a helpless-sounding voice that somehow came across as a command. Ty looked to Ryan for clarification, but all Ryan could do was shake his head in irritation. Perhaps calling Bryce would be a good thing. He'd been the first to notice Jacqueline's predatory ways, and despite his brothers' explanations of the type of personalities often found in their line of work, Bryce had steadfastly held to his own beliefs. Ryan nodded slightly, and Ty went to the communicator to track down Bryce and Matt.

"They're in their quarters," Brock told him from the control room. "I'll send them your way."

"No need," Jacqueline said sweetly, "I'll just go meet them there." She left the room before Ryan and Ty could think to stop her.

* * * *

"Hell," Bryce said as he rolled off the bed and onto his feet. Jacqueline wanting to meet them in their quarters was not a good sign. Fortunately, Matt agreed with him because they both headed for the door at the same time. If they could get into the common areas of the ship, they'd be a lot safer.

Bryce laughed softly as he realized they were essentially running from one little female, but the danger Jacqueline presented was far more than physical. None of them would ever be unfaithful to Mikayla, but Jacqueline seemed determined to undermine Mikayla's faith in her men.

Well, Bryce sure as hell wasn't going to let his wife down.

They'd barely made it halfway to the lab when Jacqueline came around the corner. The woman must've run to get there so fast. Lord knew they were both moving double-time.

"Oh," she said, looking disappointed. "I was hoping to speak to you two privately." Considering that they were the only three in that particular hallway, it should've been private enough.

"Why?" Bryce said as he crossed his arms and tried to look intimidating. Jacqueline simply ignored his body language, threaded her hand into the crook of his arm and attempted to turn him back toward their living quarters. Bryce managed to untangle himself. To hell with being polite. If the woman couldn't understand his silent signals to leave him alone, then maybe he needed to be more direct.

"I have a proposal for you two that I think you'll find very interesting." She turned to Matt and walked her fingers up his arm. Matt took a step away.

"What sort of proposal?" he asked in an annoyed voice.

"This sort of proposal," she said with what was probably supposed to be a seductive laugh. She pulled some sort of perfume bottle from her pocket, sprayed the stuff on her neck and stepped closer to them both.

Bryce felt the effects immediately. His cock hardened against his jeans, his breathing became labored, and his head filled with sensual images of fucking, claiming, marking his woman. He heard a strangled groan as the perfume—obviously made from mouse tears—affected Matt as well.

"Now," Jacqueline said as she sighed happily, "wouldn't it be more comfortable if we took this back to your quarters?"

"I have a better idea," Matt said as he lifted Jacqueline over his shoulder. For a single, suspended moment Bryce worried that his brother wasn't thinking clearly, but one look at the determination on Matt's face was enough to put his mind at ease.

Jacqueline giggled happily as Matt marched down the hallway. She wasn't quite so impressed when, after they made it to the lab in record time, Matt unceremoniously dumped Jacqueline onto one of the lab tables.

"Where is it?" Matt demanded as he ran his hands over Jacqueline's clothes trying to find the perfume bottle. Jacqueline shrieked in outrage, but Matt finally found the offensive concoction and relieved her of it.

"Call Lachlan," Bryce said in a strained voice to Ryan. "And steer clear of her," he said, pointing at Jacqueline, so angry that he didn't even want to say her name out loud. "She's wearing a perfume made from mouse tears." Ryan nodded and went straight to the communicator.

Bryce and Matt took up aggressive positions in front of both the doors. There was no way Jacqueline was leaving the room wearing a perfume designed to rob a man of his choices. Bryce ground his teeth against the need to find his wife and work off some of the strain. First he needed to contain Jacqueline, and then he needed to make sure he was in control of himself. The last thing he wanted to do was hurt his wife.

It seemed to take forever but Lachlan finally made it to the lab. He took one look at the rigid stances of the four men in the room and quickly realized the situation.

Unfortunately for Jacqueline, the woman chose that exact moment to leap off the table and have a very unladylike tantrum. Before she could shout out more than a couple of horrible threats, Lachlan threw a bucket of soapy water over her. They all watched impassively as

Jacqueline screamed like she was melting and then very inelegantly threw herself onto the floor and kicked her feet like a bratty three-year-old.

"Are you two okay?" he asked Bryce and Matt. When they shook their heads he said, "Head back to your quarters. I'll deal with this."

Bryce glanced over at Ryan and Ty, nodded his thanks to Lachlan, and turned to hurry back to their quarters. Matt was right behind him.

* * * *

Mikayla was feeling a little better just from being able to spend some time alone. Talking to Ty had helped, but he'd headed back to the lab once dinner was under control. It had been a rough few weeks for all of them, but they were almost back to Earth, and they'd soon be able to wave goodbye to the female scientists. Mikayla was humming softly when Ryan and Ty came into the room. Ryan looked pissed, and Ty looked more annoyed than she'd ever seen him. For two men who were usually joking around, it was a pretty sure sign that the close quarters were affecting everyone.

"Jacqueline kept some of the mouse tears," Ryan said immediately, his voice laced with anger. Fabulous. The woman was not only condescending and predatory in her attitude, but it would seem that she had no idea how dangerous the mouse tears really were. What the hell had she been thinking? She should've just left the dangerous cocktail on the planet. It was, after all, considered an illegal substance now.

"What happened?" Mikayla asked, concerned for all involved. After their experiences on the planet, she knew that men operating under a full dose of the mouse tears weren't in control of their own impulses.

"We managed to counteract the effects with the vitamin cocktail, but that bitch wasn't aware that we had any left," Ty said, practically grinding his teeth to dust.

"She exposed you deliberately?" Mikayla said, feeling her hackles rise. One very smart, self-involved scientist was about to get a boot up her ass.

"It's okay," Ryan said as he pulled Mikayla into his embrace. "Lachlan has already taken care of it."

"Wish I'd been there to see that," Mikayla said without any humor. "What about Misha and Keira? Were they involved?"

Ty shook his head and tried to smile reassuringly, but Mikayla could see the strain around his eyes and noticed the hard erection pressed against his pants. "They knew nothing about it. It seems that Jacqueline decided to help herself to a few of your husbands. Fortunately, Ryan and I weren't her actual targets, so we got a fairly mild dose in comparison."

"Tell me where the hell the husband-stealing bitch is so I can go scratch her eyes out." Mikayla threw the spoon she'd been holding into the sink. "Who were her actual targets?" she growled, trying to calm down even though her temper spiraled higher.

"Matt and Bryce," Ty said in a calm voice, obviously trying not to upset Mikayla any more.

"Where are they?" she demanded.

"In their quarters," Ryan said as he grabbed her hand. John stepped into the kitchen and quickly took over the dinner preparations.

Ryan and Ty both looked relieved, and the three of them practically ran from the room. "What about the others?" She could feel her heart pounding hard as her stomach twisted with anxiety. Nothing her husbands did while under the influence of such a powerful drug was their fault, but she'd be crazy to not at least try to protect them.

"Lachlan, Brock, Peter, and John were in a meeting when it all unfolded. Lachlan has the perfume Jacqueline used and is currently waiting for the bitch to stop screaming before he dumps another bucket of soapy water over her head." He grinned, but there was no humor in that smile. "None of the others got close enough to be affected."

Mikayla nodded. "What about you two?" she asked again. "Are you going to be okay?"

Ryan flashed that mischievous grin she adored and asked, "Is that an invitation to come watch?"

"Always," she said, really meaning it. She had no more secrets to tell, and she planned to keep it that way.

They finally reached the door to the room Matt and Bryce currently shared with Ryan and Ty. Mikayla noticed that Ryan unlocked the door that was usually never locked and stepped inside in front of her, obviously trying to protect her if Matt and Bryce's condition had worsened.

Fortunately, it hadn't.

Bryce and Matt looked very pleased to see her and very, very aroused but more in control than she'd expected.

"Damn," Matt muttered as he looked down at his erect cock. "It was just starting to go down, and you stepped in the door."

"I can leave," she said with a big grin on her face.

"Not a chance," Bryce said with an answering smile.

"Clothes off, Mrs. Davidson," Matt said as he stepped closer and lifted her dress over her head. He shook his head when he saw she wore a bra but quickly removed the offending garment. Her panties hit the floor a moment later.

Naked, surrounded by four of her aroused husbands, Mikayla could already feel desire winding through her, plumping her breasts, tightening her nipples, heating her pussy. Ryan and Ty lounged against the wall seemingly willing to watch, at least for the moment.

Bryce ripped his shirt over his head, threw it to the floor, and pulled her into his arms for a breath-stealing kiss. She felt Matt press naked against her back, his thick, hard cock rubbing against her crease. "I want your ass," he whispered and then began sucking on her earlobe.

"That means I get your delicious pussy," Bryce said as he dropped to his knees and arranged her legs over his shoulders. Matt balanced her from behind as Bryce licked and sucked her pussy like a man possessed. His tongue thrust hard and deep, his fingers kneading the muscles of her thighs as he gradually worked her legs wider and pushed his tongue even deeper. She was shaking, panting, begging, about to explode in orgasm when he slowed the pace and licked her leisurely.

Nearly boneless with need, Mikayla barely managed to get her hands tangled in his hair before he pulled away. Matt held her up as Bryce placed her feet on the ground. "I love you," Bryce said sincerely as he stripped off his jeans and then lifted her into his arms. He took the two steps back to the bed and then lowered onto the edge. He pulled her down, flattening her breasts against his chest and holding her still in his arms.

She wanted to squirm, still so close to orgasm that she could almost taste it. She felt Matt's hands smooth over her ass before he dipped his fingers lower and caressed her moist pussy lips. She gasped at the too soft sensation and tried to press back onto his fingers. He laughed and pressed a hand against her lower back, effectively pinning her against Bryce and making it impossible for her to move.

She moaned as Matt rubbed his cock against her slippery pussy and eased into her body. Almost as soon as he was in, he pulled back quickly and slammed in again. He grabbed her hips, holding her steady as he plunged into her over and over. She screamed as her orgasm broke and every nerve ending in her body vibrated with pleasure. Wave after wave of liquid heat drenched her veins, and she panted hard as Matt slowed his movements.

Calloused hands caressed her spine, and Mikayla felt Matt pull away. Bryce lifted her, managing to fit his cock against her still pulsing flesh and pushed into her pussy. Leisurely, he fucked her, and she gasped as cold lube landed on her anus. Matt massaged it into her back passage, his thick fingers setting her nerve endings ablaze once more.

Finally, he fit the head of his cock against her rosette and pushed past the muscle. Her ass immediately squeezed him. He growled as the grip tightened. For a moment he held still, and then he exploded into action. Bryce kept pace with his brother, thrusting harder, faster, deeper into her pussy as Matt did the same in her ass.

Breathing harshly, both Matt and Bryce seemed to be grinding their teeth. Mikayla could barely breathe as Matt used his hips and cock to press her harder between them. Her swollen clit jammed against Bryce's groin, her ass and pussy full, her body crushed between two men who loved her. Mikayla gasped as climax suddenly belted through her.

Both men groaned as her ass and pussy caressed their cocks and demanded their climax in return. They held still, and she could feel them pulsing inside her, pumping their cum deep into her body.

"I love you," Bryce whispered as Matt kissed her neck.

"So do I," Matt added.

"So do we," Ryan said from the spot where he lounged against the wall, "and right now, I think you two need to move."

Matt looked over his shoulder, and whatever he saw made him move out of the way. Bryce laughed softly as he rolled Mikayla onto her back and lifted off the bed also. Ryan and Ty advanced on her, their cocks stiff, their breathing harsh and labored.

"I need that beautiful mouth," Ty said to her as he caressed his cock.

She nodded her approval, and Ryan helped her onto her hands and knees in the middle of the bed. She licked the head of Ty's cock playfully, but he growled low in his throat and pressed harder against her mouth. Ryan thrust into her pussy in one hard lunge, jolting her and forcing Ty's cock further down her throat.

She swallowed and Ty groaned as she ran her tongue over the silky flesh of his cock. Matt and Bryce had disappeared into the bathroom to get cleaned up, but when they came back their cocks were just as hard as they'd been a few moments ago.

They stood watching as Ryan and Ty fucked her, increasing their speed as their need for her grew. Soon they were slamming into her pussy and mouth, branding her, claiming her, sending her excitement higher.

She groaned as Ty caressed her face with his hands at the same moment that Ryan pinched her clit. Orgasm burst through her, shaking every limb, as she sucked harder on Ty's cock and her pussy clenched around Ryan. Her arms shook as Ty grabbed her head, surged into her mouth, his cum pumping into her throat as Ryan swelled and hurled his seed into her pussy.

Her arms collapsed. Ty's cock fell from her mouth, but Ryan followed her down and pinned her to the bed. He kissed the back of her neck as he whispered, "Bryce and Matt need to paint you, darlin'. Shall I let them?"

She nodded. For some strange reason this always turned her on. Ryan and Ty stood back, smiling as Matt and Bryce helped her to sit on the edge of the mattress and whispered what they wanted her to do.

Practically writhing against the mattress from their dark words Mikayla opened her legs, dropped a hand to her pussy, and captured her clit between two fingers. When her men groaned in appreciation she pressed harder, teasing and flicking the hard nub until she shook on the edge of orgasm once more.

"That's it, sweetheart," Bryce encouraged. "Show us how much you want our cum."

She whimpered as heat curled through her, the eroticism of the moment overwhelming her senses. Her back arched as her fingers sped up, the wet, slippery sound joining her men's harsh breathing as Bryce and Matt neared completion.

The first hot jolt of semen hitting her breasts tipped her over the edge and she vibrated all over as climax claimed her. Each splash of warm liquid increased her pleasure, and she closed her eyes as her men groaned their orgasms.

Panting harshly, Bryce and Matt leaned over and massaged their cum into her skin.

"I love you," Matt whispered as he lifted her into his arms and carried her into the shower. She held on to him sleepily as Bryce stepped in behind them and cuddled her close. She laughed out loud when she felt two hard cocks pressing against her tired flesh.

By the time they finally left the shower, Mikayla was exhausted, sated, and very, very happy.

Epilogue

Mikayla hummed quietly as she and Peter followed their nightly ritual of doing the dishes together. It took nearly four weeks to get back to Earth, and it had affected everyone badly. Unwilling to take the cruiser and risk spending time alone with Jacqueline, Lachlan had basically been the woman's shadow for the rest of the trip. Mikayla had been very glad to finally see the woman handed over to authorities.

The station was currently in synchronous orbit over North America, but without viewing windows, Mikayla felt like she could be practically anywhere in the universe.

"Is Jacqueline all right?" she asked as Lachlan came into the kitchen.

It was probably a little silly of her to worry for a woman who'd basically tried to steal a couple of her husbands against their will, but it seemed that Jacqueline's problems weren't as clear-cut as that. The woman honestly believed she'd done nothing wrong and couldn't seem to relate her actions back to what essentially amounted to attempted rape.

Bryce and Matt had been very angry with the woman by the time the mouse tears finally wore off, and Mikayla had to acknowledge that if the mouse tears had affected women instead of men, she'd be pretty pissed and a whole lot shaken if a man had tried that on her.

"Jacqueline is currently explaining her behavior to medical personnel," Ryan said as he followed Lachlan into the kitchen. "A very small amount of the perfume she created has been preserved as evidence if she ever makes it to trial, and the rest has been dispersed into space."

"Trial?" Mikayla asked with a shudder. She really, really didn't want to find herself back in a court room again. Between all the problems Jessie Evans had created in recent years and the court case when she was seventeen, Mikayla had endured just about enough legal bullshit to last a lifetime.

"Don't worry, little one," Lachlan said. "It's very unlikely that Jacqueline's case will make it to court. The doctors are already saying that she suffers from a type of narcissistic disorder. She honestly doesn't understand what she did was wrong, and the best place for her is under medical supervision, not prison."

Mikayla nodded, hoping that was the case. If the woman was ill, then she needed treatment. It was also a relief to know that she wouldn't be doing medical research anymore. Mikayla shuddered at the thought of the damage that could be done by a person with access to medical science and no discernable conscience.

"And now for the good news," Ty said as he pulled her into his arms. "We have a new contract."

"We do?" she asked, feeling just a touch of excitement. "Where?"

Ty gave her a quick squeeze and said dramatically, "Proposed mining planet M652wd."

"Uh-huh," she said, trying to inject as much sarcasm as she could into one tiny little word. Ty and Ryan just grinned, and she finally looked to Lachlan for an explanation.

"It's a planet fairly similar to Earth. There is already a small farming colony established, so we shouldn't run into any unexpected problems from furry critters."

"Good to know," she said with more than a little relief.

"What about the rest of the station?"

"Already taken care of," Ryan said, sounding rather cocky. "We have an armed escort of mostly female soldiers, provided by the medical consortium in exchange for not suing their asses."

"We threatened to sue them?" she asked apprehensively. All this legal action was starting to wear her down.

"Of course," Ty said, sounding just as cocky as his twin. "They sent a woman with a history of unusual behavior into a dangerous situation and put lives at risk. The bad press would've been a public relations disaster, and it turned out far cheaper just to provide the escort, help us retrieve the rest of our equipment, and get us set up on a never heard of planet far away from their medical research."

Mikayla couldn't help but grin with him. In the end, the medical consortium was responsible for the behavior of their employees, and it did make sense that they should also be held accountable for fixing the mess. At least the Davidson brothers had managed to replace the canceled contract.

"So tell me about the new contract," she said, trying to sound enthusiastic. Change wasn't always bad. She had to remember that. And besides, her husbands and the station were all going with her, so it wasn't really that big a change.

As the rest of her husbands joined them in the kitchen and began discussing the details of the next planet, Mikayla took a moment to watch her men interact. They always worked as a team. Even when they disagreed, each opinion was valid and they found a way to work together.

And in that moment Mikayla felt like the luckiest woman in the universe.

It didn't matter where they were going. In the end all that mattered was that they went together. Lachlan must've seen her dreamy expression because he pulled her into his embrace and whispered all the things he planned to do on the trip to the new planet.

Yes, change could be good.

Especially when it was *that* inspiring.

End of
A Bride for Eight Brothers, Volume 2

To be continued in
A Bride for Eight Brothers, Volume 3

ABOUT THE AUTHOR

Abby Blake prefers to read or write romance over just about everything else—except maybe chocolate. Most days she can be found hurrying to do what needs to be done so that she can curl up with her laptop and her latest bunch of heroes.

Visit her website at www.abbyblake.webs.com.

Also by Abby Blake

Siren LoveXtreme Forever: A Bride for Eight Brothers 1:
Mikayla's Men
Siren LoveXtreme Forever: A Bride for Eight Brothers 2:
Sweet Captivation
Siren LoveXtreme Forever: A Bride for Eight Brothers 5:
Hot Inspiration
Siren LoveXtreme Forever: A Bride for Eight Brothers 6:
Mikayla's Family
Ménage Everlasting: Altered Destinies 1: *Lost*
Ménage Everlasting: Altered Destinies 2: *Runner*
Ménage Everlasting: Altered Destinies 3: *Hidden*
Ménage Everlasting: Altered Destinies 4: *Stolen*
Ménage Everlasting: Altered Destinies 5: *Soldier*
Ménage Everlasting: Altered Destinies 6: *Traitor*
Ménage Everlasting: Viper's Dungeon 1: *Emma's Education*
Ménage Everlasting: *Fire*

Available at
BOOKSTRAND.COM

Siren Publishing, Inc.
www.SirenPublishing.com

Lightning Source UK Ltd.
Milton Keynes UK
UKOW031403141111

182049UK00009B/72/P